Dawn and Whitney, Friends Forever

Dawn and Whitney, Friends Forever
Ann M. Martin

AN
APPLE
PAPERBACK

SCHOLASTIC INC.
New York Toronto London Auckland Sydney

*The author gratefully acknowledges
Nola Thacker
for her help in
preparing this manuscript.*

Cover art by Hodges Soileau

ISBN 0-590-48221-1

12 11 10 9 8 7 6 5 4 3   4 5 6 7 8 9/9

Printed in the U.S.A.   40

First Scholastic printing, August 1994

CHAPTER 1

Sunny, sunny California.

That's redundant. (Check out those vocab words). What it means is, you don't need to say that the sun is always shining in California. Just the word California says it all.

Do I sound as if I like living here? I do. Maybe it's no coincidence, either, that my father's nickname for me is Sunshine. Or that one of my two best friends in California is named Sunny.

And summer in California is California to the max. Surf's up. Minimum clothing dress code. Sunscreen and shades and . . . well, you get the idea.

Dawn Schafer (that's me) of Stoneybrook, Connecticut and Palo City, California, was about to settle in for a smooooth summer in the redundantly sunny California sun. (Oh, okay, California isn't *always* sunny and warm, but it feels that way to me.)

I guess I do sound a little like a tourist, the ones you see on the beaches sometimes with cameras and big flowered shirts and weird sunglasses, snapping pictures of everything that moves. But I was actually born and raised in California. I never truly appreciated it, though, until my mother and father got divorced and my mom moved back to her hometown, Stoneybrook, Connecticut, with me and my younger brother, Jeff. That's where her parents, our grandparents, Granny and Pop-Pop, still live.

Naturally I was not enthusiastic about the move. But we bought this old farmhouse built back in the 1700s and I actually discovered a secret passageway from my bedroom to the barn. Then I made friends with Mary Anne Spier and she invited me to join a group called the Baby-sitters Club (or the BSC) and soon I was pretty happy.

Not my brother Jeff, though. He went from obnoxious-but-lovable little brother to monster brother and he even started getting in trouble at school. He wanted to go back to California and eventually, Mom and Dad decided that it might be best.

I hated to see Jeff go. In such a short time we'd gone from being a family of four in one place, to a bicoastal divorced family, two here, two there.

2

But not for long. Mary Anne's father and my mother rediscovered each other. They'd known each other in high school and dated and then lost touch. But the romance rekindled and they got married. (Mary Anne's mother had died when she was just a baby and she and her father had been a family of two for practically her whole life.) So anyway, Mary Anne and her father moved into the farmhouse along with Mary Anne's gray tiger kitten Tigger. Since Mary Anne and I were already best friends, things couldn't get any better than that, right?

Wrong.

I kept on missing Dad and Jeff. And the harder I tried not to miss them, the worse it got. Not California. I mean, I missed it, but I could live without it. My father and my brother were a different story, though. I finally decided I had to go west again for more than a visit.

It was a hard decision. It made Mary Anne cry (which made me cry, too), and it made Mom pretty miserable, especially since she took it personally. But eventually she and Dad worked it out (along with the guidance counselors at Stoneybrook Middle School and at Vista, my California school, who had to make sure I would have "continuity of education" if I moved back to California for any length of time). And I came back to Palo City for a good, long stay.

The right decision. A hard decision, but the right one. I'll be going back to Stoneybrook before too much longer but, right now, I'm enjoying every minute of the west coast part of my bicoastal life.

Well, almost every minute.

It's this dating thing, you see.

I mean, there are plenty of nice people out here, but . . .

Oh, I'm not talking about *me*! I mean our father. You see, he's been dating a lot lately. Especially since he broke his engagement with Carol, this woman he'd been seeing for a long time. I admit, I was relieved when they broke up. Not that I didn't like Carol. But she tried *so* hard to be cool that it left me cold. I realize now that I didn't understand how hard it must have been for Carol, too, coming into a ready-made family and trying to fit in. Worse than being the new kid in school by about a hundred times.

But anyway, that's over and Dad is doing what Granny calls "playing the field." That means he's dating a lot. And a lot of different kinds of people.

It also means that after the first couple of dates, the "date me, date my kids" theme goes into effect. That means that on the next date, Dad includes Jeff and me.

Try to imagine going on a date — which includes your parents. Pretty weird, huh?

Well, it must be pretty weird for dad and his dates, too. I'm glad he wants us to like the people he goes out with. But I keep thinking there must be an easier way . . .

"What's for dinner?" Jeff powered through the kitchen on his way to his next rendezvouz with chaos, and I snagged a loop of his jeans.

"Endive salad, three-cheese macaroni, asparagus, and raspberry crisp," I said. "And you're in charge of setting the table."

"Endive?" Jeff clutched his throat and Mrs. Bruen, our housekeeper, laughed.

"You've never had endive, Jeff," Mrs. Bruen said. It was true. Jeff just liked giving me grief, little-brother style.

Jeff let go of his throat and I let go of his jeans and a cunning look came into his eyes. "Hey," he said.

I recognized the look, a holdover from his most recent career plan to become a comedian, which meant that he told a zillion bad jokes to anybody who was unwary enough to stand still for one second.

I groaned, but Jeff went on. "Hey, Dawn, Mrs. Bruen, what did the dog say when they served it endive?"

5

Mrs. Bruen smiled good-naturedly. "I don't know, Jeff. What did the dog say?"

"Barf, barf!" shouted Jeff.

I had to smile at that one. "That's terrible," I said. "But it's not bad."

Jeff looked enormously pleased with himself.

Just then the doorbell rang.

"Does Dad have a date?" Jeff asked.

"Yeah," I said. "But it's too early. That must be Sunny. She's sleeping over tonight."

I wiped my hands on a kitchen towel, put the raspberry crisp in a safe place on the counter, ready to pop into the oven when we sat down for dinner, and headed for the door.

"Dawn!" cried Sunny, as if we hadn't talked on the phone only a couple of hours before.

I've known Sunshine Daydream Winslow longer than I've known anybody else in my whole life (except my mother and father and my grandparents, of course). Her parents, as you might guess from Sunny's name, were (and still are, I guess) hippies. The Winslows live down the street from us and Mrs. Winslow is a potter, an artist and a really nice human being. Come to think of it, she's a lot like another artist I know, a fellow member of the BSC back in Stoneybrook, Claudia Kishi. But more about that later.

"Sunny!" I exclaimed now, matching her

tone and grinning. Sunny bounded in, slung her backpack into the nearest corner and sniffed appreciatively. "What's cooking? It smells like one of my main foods."

"Three-cheese macaroni." It's a Mrs. Bruen specialty and it *is* one of Sunny's favorites.

"Super!" exclaimed Sunny.

"Yeah, I like it, too," I told her.

Sunny and I are a lot alike. Not only is her name the same as my nickname, but we are both blonde, although Sunny is a strawberry-blonde and my hair is almost white. We also like natural food and don't eat red meat, and we're independent, outgoing, and easy going. We like to surf. We *love* ghost stories.

"I'm starved," said Sunny as we headed back for the kitchen.

"You're just in time. Jeff's setting the table now." I raised my voice so Jeff, who I could see edging out of the kitchen, could hear me.

Jeff stopped. Then he went over to the silverware drawer and scooped up a handful of knives, forks, and spoons and headed for the dining room.

"Hey, Jeff-man," said Sunny. "How's it going?"

Jeff stopped. That cunning look came into his eyes. "Hey, Sunny. Listen, what did the dog — "

"Table first, jokes second," I intervened

quickly. "And you know what, Jeff? You should wait till Dad gets here. Then he can hear your joke, too."

"Okay," said Jeff. He took one of the dinner knives, stuck it under his arm, cried, "I've been *stuck*," and reeled away.

Mrs. Bruen rolled her eyes.

"Anything I can do to help?" asked Sunny.

"It's all done," said Mrs. Bruen, popping open the oven and pulling out the casserole.

Jeff came back in, grabbed the plates, and hustled out. This time he didn't waste time cutting up. Everything smelled too good.

It *was* good, too. Our father came in and sat at the table with us (although he couldn't eat; he was going to take his latest date to dinner after a movie). Jeff got to tell his barf, barf joke again. And Sunny and I laughed a lot and settled down to concentrate on macaroni and asparagus.

"What movie are you going to see, Mr. Schafer?" Sunny asked.

"We're going to a Charlie Chaplin film festival," my father said.

"That sounds cool," said Sunny.

"Could be," said my father. He winked at me and I tried to smile encouragingly.

"You'll have a good time," I said. Then I thought, good grief, I sound just like someone's parents. The next thing I know, I'll be telling Dad just to be himself.

Dad added to the feeling by saying as he stood up to go, "Do I look okay?"

"Super," said Sunny, and I nodded.

"See you guys later, then," my father said.

"We'll save you some dessert," answered Jeff. "Ha, ha."

After dinner was over (and Jeff had, despite his best efforts, not eaten all the raspberry crisp), and Mrs. Bruen had left, Sunny and I were the baby-sitters in charge, informally.

We followed Jeff out into the yard. Half a dozen kids were out in their yards around us, or zooming up and down the sidewalks on blades and bicycles. But when Jeff said, "Soccer," it wasn't long before we had a pick-up game of soccer organized, with Sunny and me playing goalie at either end. It was fun, kind of like the Krushers' softball games back in Stoneybrook. (The Krushers are a softball team made up of kids of all ages — the average age is 5.8.) Everyone played hard but fair and when Jeff scored a goal on me and shouted, "Goallllll, Schafer," everyone cheered good-naturedly along with him.

When it got too dark for that, we headed back inside and settled in for a movie. Not too much later, I noticed that Jeff's eyes were closing. Sunny and I exchanged a look. We knew better than to suggest that Jeff might be getting sleepy. He's ten and a little touchy about being treated "like a baby."

"I'm getting tired," I said to Sunny, but looking at Jeff.

She knew exactly what I meant. She stretched and yawned and said, "Me, too."

Jeff opened his eyes, squinted at the screen for a moment, then said, "Me, too. See you guys."

"I'll come tell you good night in a little while," I said.

"Okay," said Jeff.

"Brush your teeth," I called after him.

"Okay."

"So how sleepy *are* you?" asked Sunny.

"Not," I said. "Besides, it's not *that* late." How late was it in Connecticut? I wondered.

Sunny, my oldest-friend-and-mind-reader, asked, "How late is it in Connecticut? Not too late for a phone call, right?"

I flashed her a grin. "Right!"

A few minutes later (three hours later in Connecticut), I heard Mary Anne's voice on the phone.

"Dawn! It's you! Where are you?"

"California still," I said.

Mary Anne laughed. "And we still miss you in Stoneybrook. What's happening?" We

10

talked for a little while. I updated her on my father's new dating plan and what was happening in the We ♥ Kids Club (which is the more laid back California version of the Babysitters Club back in Stoneybrook), and she told me what was happening with the BSC. We didn't talk too long — after all, if my father had a mondo phone bill, he might object to my calling Connecticut so much — but it was long enough to be satisfying.

Afterward, I went to say good night to Jeff, which turned out to be unnecessary, and by the time I got back to help Sunny make popcorn, Dad was coming home from his date.

"How was it?" I said as he walked into the kitchen.

"The popcorn was good," said Dad.

"And?" asked Sunny.

"I liked the movie. *The Gold Rush*. It's one of my favorite Chaplin films."

"And?" I prompted.

"That's it," said my Dad.

"You have to kiss a lot of frogs before you can find a prince. Or a princess," said Sunny.

"What!" I shrieked. I've known Sunny forever. But I've never heard her say that.

Sunny turned bright red.

My father burst out laughing. "Thanks for the advice, Sunny. And I know you're right. Some day my frog princess will come."

11

My father was still laughing as he headed for his room.

And I was still giving Sunny major grief for that line when we went to sleep late that night, after talking through one and a half scary movies and eating another bowl of popcorn.

CHAPTER 2

"This meeting of the We Love Kids Club will now come to order," I intoned.

Silence.

I looked around the room.

Sunny's mouth dropped open.

Maggie Blume gave a theatrical little gasp.

Jill Henderson looked at me with real concern in her chocolate brown eyes and said, "Dawn? Are you feeling okay?"

I couldn't help it. I burst out laughing. After a moment, Sunny and Maggie started laughing, too, and Jill grinned sheepishly.

The reason they were laughing was because that was definitely *not* the way we run our club. Sunny started the W♥KC when I was in Stoneybrook, after I told her about the Baby-sitters Club I'd joined there.

The BSC is still going strong in Stoneybrook and I'm still a member. (Basically.) And every Monday, Wednesday, and Friday afternoon from five-thirty to six (Stoneybrook time) I can tell you exactly what my closest friends and fellow BSC members are doing. They're sitting in Claudia Kishi's room having a BSC meeting. Kristy Thomas is the president and one of the founding members of the BSC. She got the idea one night while listening to her mother make a zillion phone calls trying to find a baby-sitter for her little brother. What, Kristy the idea queen thought, what if a person could make just one phone call and reach several baby-sitters at once?

Now at exactly five-thirty Stoneybrook time, Kristy is sitting in her director's chair with her green visor on, saying, "This meeting of the BSC will now come to order." Claudia, the vice-president, is passing around the junk food that she keeps hidden in strategic places in her room. Mary Anne, who is BSC secretary, is keeping the record book. Stacey McGill, the treasurer, is collecting and counting dues (if it is Monday, dues day). Shannon, who is (alternate) officer (and my replacement), and responsible for taking over someone else's job in case of emergency, is there. And Jessica Ramsey and Mallory Pike, who are junior officers (they can't sit at night because they are younger), are there too, talking and laughing and taking care of business.

Which is not exactly the way the We ♥ Kids

Club works, as you might have guessed.

We're more laid back. Easygoing.

But not *too* easy going. That almost got us into trouble not too long ago. Our club got written up in the newspaper and then we were featured on a local news station on TV and the next thing we knew, we were swamped with calls. Our, er, loose organizational style meant that we ended up double booking and overbooking and almost making a real mess out of our business. That's when we decided that laid back didn't mean no rules at all. So we made up a few.

1. Regular meeting times. Every week. At Sunny's.

2. Keep a record book.

Are you waiting for more rules? That's it. No officers. No other special rules. Unless, of course, we decide we need them.

I looked around the room at my fellow club members, thought about the BSC, and wondered if we'd ever have a BSC / W♥KC convention.

Hmmm. That would be a job for Kristy Thomas. Kristy is the most organized person in the world, and possibly the universe. She lives with her mother and stepfather, a step-brother and stepsister (part time), her maternal grandmother, her three brothers (two older, one younger), her adopted little sister, a dog, a cat, and a family ghost in a mansion in Stoneybrook. The mansion and the stepfather and stepsiblings came along after her mother recently remarried. Before that, Kristy's mother was working pretty hard as a single parent to raise four kids. (Kristy's father left when her seven-year-old brother was just a baby and is now rarely in touch).

Kristy has brown hair and brown eyes and is the shortest person in her class. She's a casual dresser, jeans and sweaters mostly, but that's the only thing she is casual about. As I said before, Kristy is *intensely* organized. She not only thought of the BSC and got it going, but she also thought of the BSC record book, complete with client list and a calendar of each member's sitting jobs (no double booking or overbooking in the BSC!). Club members also keep notes and records of their various jobs in the BSC notebook, which all the members use as a sort of reference to keep them posted on what's happening with the kids they take care of.

Mary Anne is Kristy's oldest and best friend, a classic case of opposites attracting, at least personality-wise. Mary Anne and Kristy sort of look alike — they're both short and have brown hair and are pretty conservative dressers — but Mary Anne is quiet and very shy and sensitive, while Kristy is outspoken and

16

opinionated and occasionally thick-skinned. I've almost never seen Kristy cry, but it doesn't take much to bring tears to Mary Anne's eyes. Her boyfriend, Logan, knows to be prepared when they go to movies that have the least possibility of being sad.

Mary Anne is also my best friend in Stoneybrook and my stepsister, and I think she is a super excellent friend and sister, *especially* sister. After her mother died, her father raised her very strictly (he wanted to be sure he did things right) and I think that's one of the reasons she is such a terrific sister. She'd never had a brother or sister or a mom before. So when our parents got married and we made up a whole new family, it was a whole new, special thing for Mary Anne in even more ways than it was for me.

Anyway, I miss her patience and the way she listens and how supportive she is, and how stubborn she can be about something she believes in. I know Mary Anne misses me, too, and we try to stay in close touch.

I like to imagine her at the meetings, keeping the record book — and keeping Kristy and the other BSC members in line!

Claudia? Well, she's one of the original members of the BSC and the only member with her own phone line, which is the reason the meetings are at her house in her room.

(That and quick access to junk food!) Claud is an artist and someday she's going to be world-famous. But right now she does her art, keeps her look super-cool and uniquely Claudia-esque (she's Japanese-American, with dark eyes and long black hair), and tries not to be bothered by the fact that school work is mostly a mystery to her. Claudia has a genius older sister who thrives on school, but maybe Claudia's beginning to realize, deep down, that she's a genius too, in her own way — an artistic one.

Stacey McGill is Claud's best friend and the BSC treasurer. She was born and raised in New York City, which gives her a distinct "city" style. She moved to Stoneybrook with her parents, moved back to NYC with her parents, then moved to Stoneybrook *again* with her mom after her parents got divorced. Stacey's a math whiz. She's got long blonde hair (darker than mine), is an only child (like Mary Anne) and, like me, watches what she eats. But Stacey does it because she really has too. She has diabetes, which means her blood sugar level can go haywire. She has to be very careful with her diet and inject herself every day with insulin.

Jessica Ramsey and Mallory Pike are sixth-graders and junior club members, best friends, and talented, too. Jessi is a ballerina who is already taking special classes, while Mallory writes and illustrates her own stories. Both Jessi and Mallory are the oldest in their families. Jessi is the oldest of three kids, and Mal is the oldest of *eight*, which means she came to the BSC with plenty of experience. In fact, her family was and is one of the BSC's biggest clients. Mallory has pale white skin with freckles, red hair, glasses, and braces. Jessi has medium brown skin, brown eyes, and loooong legs. Mal and Jessi are crazy about horses.

Logan, Mary Anne's boyfriend, is the other associate member (actually, the only one, now that I'm in California and Shannon is filling in for me). He doesn't attend meetings all that often, but he takes occasional jobs when we can't handle them all. Shannon Kilbourne, who has my job now, used to be an associate member, too. She's Kristy's neighbor and the only BSC member who goes to a private school, Stoneybrook Day School. She's a bit like Kristy — involved in everything, and organized enough to make it look easy.

A baby-sitters convention. Would it ever happen? And what would it be like?

The phone beeped and we stopped laughing, and Sunny, who was closest to the phone, picked it up. "We Love Kids Club," she said.

And that was how *our* meetings usually came to order.

It was the day after Sunny had slept over at my house and we were at a regular meeting of the We ♥ Kids Club.

I looked around the room at my fellow club members. We are all blonde: I'm the palest, with white blonde hair. Sunny's a strawberry blonde. Maggie's got short golden blonde hair (with purple raccoon streaks over each ear today, to match the long tail of blonde hair braided with purple string hanging down her back). And Jill has dark golden hair.

We're all health food fans, too. But that doesn't mean we don't eat snacks at our meetings, too. Our snacks just tend toward the fruits and nuts and yogurt variety instead of potato chips and brownies and sugar-frosted cereal (yes, Claudia's been known to eat sugar-frosted cereal right out of the box).

Sunny put her hand over the receiver and announced the job. We all looked at each other, and Maggie said, "I can do it. I think."

Jill pulled out the record book from under a stack of books on Sunny's desk and tossed it across the room to Maggie, who flipped through. She ran her finger down the page.

"Yup, no prob," said Maggie, scrawling her name and the time on the date.

Sunny nodded and got back on the phone to confirm.

See? Much more casual than the BSC.

Maggie traded the record book for our version of the club notebook — our own personal health food cookbook. "I know there was a recipe for tofu-vegetable skewers in here somewhere," she muttered.

"A cookout?" asked Sunny, suddenly focusing. (Food is our favorite shared interest).

"Yeah." Maggie shrugged. "My dad has some people coming in from Hollywood and he's doing this cookout thing." She wrinkled her nose. "I *think* snails are involved." We all shrieked and began making gross suggestions as Maggie flipped through the book.

Maggie wasn't kidding — about the snails or Hollywood. Her father is in the movie business and stars go in and out of her house. And she lives in a mansion, too. It's California-style, with a landscaped pool (natural shape, not square), a screening room, a gym, and dozens and dozens of rooms. Her kitchen is so big you could Rollerblade in it.

But to Maggie, it isn't a big deal. It's not that she's trying to be super-cool and pretend it doesn't matter. It's just that she's used to it, I guess.

Maggie keeps her hair short and punkish (as you might have guessed from my description of it) with clothes to match, like a favorite leather bomber jacket that she wears rain, shine, hot, cold. She'd brought it with her today, over a black cropped tank top, leopard leggings, and lace-up black boots.

Jill reached over and pointed. "You just passed the recipe, Mag."

"Oh, right."

Jill smiled. "Snails," she said. "Ugh." And then, "Poor snails . . ."

She was only half kidding. Jill is probably the most serious of us, and she's sensitive in ways that remind me of Mary Anne sometimes. Jill lives with her mom and older sister Liz in the hills at the edge of town, along with three huge boxers: Spike, Shakespeare, and Smee. She's the only one of us who doesn't live in the neighborhood and she usually takes a bus to meetings. Like the rest of us, Jill likes to surf. And she is seriously good at it, too.

The phone rang again and Jill picked it up. "We Love Kids Club," she said. The little smile on her face turned into a serious expression as she listened. "Oh," she said. "Mmm. Well, we need to check our schedule book. We'll call you right back."

We all looked at Jill in surprise as she wrote down the caller's name and phone number and hung up the phone.

"Whoa," said Sunny. "What was *that* all about?"

"A new client. Mr. Cater," Jill said.

"New clients are good," said Maggie en-

22

couragingly. "What's the prob? A problem child? We can handle it."

"No. No, not a problem child." Jill looked around and said, "His daughter's name is Whitney. Mr. Cater wants a sitter/companion for her for the next few weeks."

"A long-term job. That's good." Sunny leaned over and fished for the record book.

"She's twelve," said Jill.

That stopped us.

"Twelve?" I asked. "She's almost our age!"

"She's been attending a special school with a summer program, but she's leaving the summer program because she's about to be switched out of her old school and into the public school system. Her parents have found a day camp for Whitney and they're going to take off alternate mornings for the next few weeks until the camp begins. But they need a sitter for the afternoons.

Jill paused, then added, "Whitney has Down's syndrome."

There was a little silence, then Maggie said, "Like Corky, right? In that TV show."

"Yeah," said Jill.

"Okay," said Sunny. "It's a long job. Does anybody want to take on the whole thing, every afternoon? Or do we want to split it up?"

"I'll take it," I said. "Unless someone else . . . ?"

Maggie said, "I would, but I can't do the whole thing. Having just one person on the job might be easier. But I'd like to be counted as your substitute if you can't make it someday or something."

"Done deal," said Sunny, handing the record book to me.

I took it and Jill handed me the phone number and Mr. Cater's name.

I called Mr. Cater back at his office.

"Good," he said. "Let me write that down in my book. Dawn Schafer." He gave me the details and concluded. "Whitney will be pleased, I think. We've decided to tell her you're a new friend, rather than a baby-sitter. She feels she doesn't need a baby-sitter, especially now that she's graduating to public school."

"Great," I said. "I'll see you then."

I hung up the phone, intrigued and pleased with my new job and with the prospect of steady work for several weeks to come.

CHAPTER 3

The Caters didn't live far from our house, so I walked there the first afternoon I was supposed to baby-sit for Whitney.

Baby-sit? No, it wasn't exactly the right word. I had talked to both Mr. and Mrs. Cater several times since taking the job and although I hadn't actually met them, I felt as if I knew them, and Whitney, too.

I admit, I had been a little worried at first, even though the job had intrigued me. I had never met anyone with Down's syndrome before and I wasn't sure quite what to expect. I didn't think it would be the same as the baby-sitting job Kristy had had, back in Stoneybrook, with an autistic girl named Susan, who never spoke or even seemed to pay attention to what was going on around her. (Although she could play just about any piece of music on the piano after hearing it only once.) Some specialists thought Susan was retarded, although no one was sure. And no one, not even the specialists, knew what caused Susan's disability.

No one knows why children with Down's syndrome are born the way they are, either, according to Mr. Cater.

"It's a congenital defect," he said. "That means it develops before birth. It's caused by a chromosome abnormality, the appearance of a certain chromosome three times instead of twice in some or all of the cells. No one knows why it happens."

"Oh," I said. At that point, I didn't understand much more than I had before.

Mr. Cater went on. "Practically speaking, it means that Whitney is retarded. She's not very retarded. Many people with Down's syndrome aren't. And she doesn't have any extreme manifestations of physical traits commonly associated with Down's syndrome, such as retarded growth or impaired coordination, or thank God, a heart condition. It's one of the reasons we feel that Whitney will be able to mainstream fairly easily, relatively speaking. Of course, she'll continue to take some special courses, and to work with specialists, like her speech therapist."

"Oh," I said again. I understood a little more of what Mr. Cater had said this time, but I didn't know how to ask him what I really wanted to find out: what was Whitney like?

I smiled as I walked down the street, remembering what had happened next. Mr. Cater had cleared his throat and said, "Perhaps you should speak to Annette. My wife. I'll have her call you when she gets home from work."

Mrs. Cater had called soon after. What she told me had been less technical and more specific.

"Whitney is so excited about going to a new school," she'd said, right away. "And so excited about meeting a new friend."

"About that. The new friend story," I'd said. "Are you sure that's what you want to tell her?" Somehow, the idea made me uncomfortable. I'd never lied to anyone I'd sat with before.

"That's what we *have* told her. That you are a new friend. As my husband may have explained to you, Whitney's pride would be hurt if we told her we'd hired a baby-sitter. After all, she is twelve years old!" Mrs. Cater laughed.

"I can understand *that*," I said, remembering how hard some of us (such as Mary Anne) had worked to convince our parents that we weren't little kids any more, that we could make decisions on our own and handle more grown-up responsibility. But even though I could understand, I wanted to say more. However, Mrs. Cater didn't give me a chance.

"Good," she said emphatically. "Anyway, Whitney is easygoing. She likes to laugh. She's a good listener. She's very sympathetic and sensitive to others' moods. She's friendly and outgoing and although she is retarded, she's mildly retarded. I don't think you'll find her too different from any of your other baby-sitting charges, ultimately."

"Okay," I said. "Sounds great."

We had worked out the details of my first visit, and hung up.

Ooops! I'd been so busy thinking that I'd almost walked right past the Caters' house. I backtracked a few steps, hoping no one was watching, and headed for the front door. The Caters opened the door almost as soon as I'd knocked.

"Hello," I said. "I'm Dawn Schafer from the We Love Kids Club."

"Of course," said the woman. "I'm Annette Cater and this is my husband, James."

"Hello, Mrs. Cater. Hello, Mr. Cater."

"Come in," said Mrs. Cater, stepping back.

I stepped in, then followed the Caters down a broad hall to a large sunny room at the back of the house.

"Whitney is folding her laundry and putting it away," explained Mrs. Cater. "She'll be here in a minute. I told her it was important to have a clean room for her guest."

"Oh." I said, trying to remember the last time I'd cleaned up my room when Sunny or anyone had come over.

"I'm going in to my office this afternoon," said Mrs. Cater. "James is here on his lunch hour, so we'll both be leaving shortly. There is a list over by the phone of our office numbers, emergency numbers, and neighbors' names and numbers if anything should come up."

"Great," I said. We baby-sitters love it when parents are prepared like that. Surprisingly, not all parents always are. I was about to ask if Whitney had any rules I should know about, or any special foods she should or shouldn't eat, allergies or medications I should know about, but Mr. Cater beat me to it.

"Whitney is prone to ear infections," he said. "She has to wear special ear plugs when she goes swimming and put drops in before and after. Other than that, she has no allergies or anything that you need to worry about." He paused, then smiled. "Except she does have a sweet tooth."

I was about to ask if Whitney had any games or special things she liked to do, but Mrs. Cater looked past me toward the door and said brightly, "Whitney. Here's Dawn. She's come to keep you company this afternoon while we're at work."

I stood up and turned around to see a short, somewhat stocky girl standing in the door of the room. She had straight brown hair and brown eyes that seemed to slant slightly at the corners. Her face was round and she had a short nose. As she stood there looking at me, she didn't change expression at all.

I smiled. "Hi, Whitney."

Whitney's face immediately broke into a wide grin and she said, "Hi, Dawn! That's a pretty name."

"Thank you," I said. Whitney's voice was low, almost hoarse, and she spoke carefully.

Whitney came toward me and held out her hand. "How do you do?" she asked.

Smiling inwardly at this lesson in manners that Whitney was so obviously practicing, I took her hand. "Fine, thank you. How are you?"

"Fine, thank you," said Whitney. Then she burst out, "I want earrings, too."

I could tell the Caters had heard that before. "When the right time comes, dear," said Mr. Cater, standing up. He bent to kiss the top of Whitney's head. "Your mother and I are going to work while Dawn stays here. We'll be back at six."

"Good-bye," said Whitney. She was staring intently at my ears. Then she said triumphantly, "You have *four* earrings, Dawn. I want four earrings."

"I'm thirteen," I said quickly. "Maybe when you're my age, you can get earrings."

Mrs. Cater smiled and patted her daughter's shoulder. "See you in a little while, Whitney. There's juice in the refrigerator if you want something to drink, Dawn. And help yourself to whatever you want in the kitchen. But don't let Whitney spoil her appetite for dinner."

I was worried for a moment that Mrs. Cater's instructions would sound too much like she was leaving me in charge, like a babysitter, but Whitney didn't seem to notice. She looked up at her parents and said, "Good-bye, Mom. Good-bye, Dad."

A few minutes later, the Caters were gone.

"What a beautiful day," I said. "What do you want to do?"

In answer, Whitney caught my hand and pulled me out into the hall.

"Where are we going, Whitney?" I asked.

"To my room," explained Whitney. "It's *clean*."

"That's great. I'm not so good about cleaning up my room. But if *I'm* bad, you should see my brother Jeff! The messes he makes are *awesome*. My father just closes the door sometimes and says as long as he can't smell anything, he's assuming it's okay."

Whitney nodded, almost absently, and flung the door of her room open proudly. "Look!" she said.

I wasn't sure what I expected to see, but it was a typical girl's room, decorated in green and white and soft peach. A big canopy bed stood in the middle of the room with a patchwork quilt across the foot. A wide desk with a chair was by the window, and next to it was a comfortable looking armchair. Bookshelves lined one wall and on the other wall was a big poster of seals cavorting in the ocean.

"You like the water," I said, remembering what Mr. Cater had said.

"I'm a good swimmer," answered Whitney. "See?" She pointed to the bookshelves and I realized that many of the shelves contained trophies.

"Wow," I said. "Did you win all these?"

Whitney nodded. "At my school. We have swim meets every year."

"That's great, Whitney!" I said.

"Do you like to swim?" asked Whitney.

"I sure do," I answered. "And surf."

Whitney's eyes lit up. "In the ocean?" She thought for a minute, then said. "A-awesome."

I laughed.

Whitney laughed, too. Then she squatted and pulled a stack of magazines out from the bottom of her bookshelf.

"What's that?" I asked.

"Magazines. M-my mother's," explained Whitney.

I sat down on the floor and Whitney straightened her legs out slowly and sat next to me. She opened the magazines and pointed to a picture of Keanu Reeves.

"He's cute."

"Yeah," I agreed. "Very."

"You think he's cute?"

"Yup. But I like him better." I pointed to the photo of another star. Whitney studied him seriously, her head turned to one side and her tongue sticking out slightly from between her lips.

Then she said, "No. I like Keanu better."

"Well, I like what he's wearing better," I said.

Whitney nodded and turned the page. She studied the picture for a moment and then said, "*He* has earrings, too."

I laughed and shook my head. "Soon you'll have them, too. Your parents just want you to be more grown-up."

"I *am* grown-up!" Whitney exclaimed.

"Yeah, but parents never believe you are.

You have to show them," said Dawn.

Whitney thought for a moment, then nodded. Then she said, "Do you have a boyfriend?"

"No. Not right now. Do you?" asked Dawn.

Whitney giggled and put her hand over her mouth. "No. Not yet." Her eyes lit on my backpack, which I'd dropped on the floor next to me.

"Do you have magazines in there?" she asked, pointing.

"No. It's mostly empty," I answered.

"May I look inside?"

"Sure," I said, sliding the backpack over to her. She opened it and my string shopping bag fell out.

"What's this?" she asked.

"It's a string bag," I said. "I carry it with me wherever I go so that if I buy anything, I can put it in there instead of in a plastic bag. Plastic bags are bad for the environment."

Whitney nodded, but her attention had been caught by something else. "Oooh, make-up!" She pulled out a tube of clear pink sunscreen lip gloss and held it up admiringly. "May I try it on, Dawn? Please?"

"Of course," I said.

Whitney scrambled to her feet and went over to the small mirror that hung above her chest of drawers. She opened the lip gloss with great care. Drawing her eyebrows together in a frown, she leaned forward and meticulously outlined her lips with the gloss.

"It looks nice," I said, coming to stand beside her. Our two faces looked back at us from the mirror: mine tan, with a faint dusting of freckles, my hair straight and white-blonde on either side of my face, Whitney's face pale and round with her short dark hair and flat, immobile features. But then she smiled and I didn't think she looked so expressionless after all. Or so different.

I decided it was like getting to know anybody new. At first, new people look strange because, well, they are strangers. But after that you know them and then they just look like themselves.

"Nice," repeated Whitney. She nodded in satisfaction, closed the tube of gloss with equal care and handed it ceremoniously back to me. "Thank you, Dawn."

"You're welcome," I said. I walked over to my backpack and put the gloss back in and sat down. "So, what else do you do besides swim? Do you have other favorite sports? Or hobbies?"

Whitney thought for a moment, then said, "I like animals. I like bears. And seals. I want to get a job, too. I'd like to baby-sit and earn money of my own."

"That's what I do to earn money," I said. "Some friends of mine and I have our own baby-sitting business, the We Love Kids Club."

"Really? Do you earn lots of money?"

"Well, not exactly," I answered. "But we do a lot of work. Being a good baby-sitter is a big responsibility. I've even taken a class to learn how to be a better baby-sitter."

Whitney asked me what seemed like a million questions about my job. We sat on her floor and laughed and talked until I heard the front door open and Mr. Cater's voice call, "Whitney? Dawn?"

I headed home feeling pretty good. Whitney was nice. And fun. And funny. I'd enjoyed this job a lot, and I was looking forward to seeing Whitney again the next afternoon.

CHAPTER 4

"I don't like that color." Whitney held a magazine up for me to inspect. A boy in an olive green T-shirt and a black zebra print jacket smiled out at us from the page. Whitney pointed to the model's shirt.

"Yeah," I said. "He's cute, but that color green is major yuck. At least, it would look terrible on me. I look better in summer colors."

Whitney switched her attention from the model to me. "Summer colors?" she asked.

"Yeah. You know, the colors you usually see in the summer: bright blue skies, bright yellow sun. Those are the colors that look best on me. But other people look better in colors from other seasons of the year. I have a friend in Connecticut, Mallory, and she has red hair and pale skin and freckles. She looks really good in autumn colors, like the autumn leaf colors. You know, orange-red and gold. Like that."

Whitney frowned. Then she said, "What colors am I?"

I studied her for a moment, her brown eyes and dark hair. Then I said, "Maybe spring. Spring green and all the colors of the spring flowers."

"I like that," said Whitney. "Spring. Spring colors. You are summer and I am spring."

"Yeah," I said, grinning.

Whitney flipped through a couple more magazines, talking about the different colors. It was interesting to look at magazines that way, as if I were learning different colors in a whole new way. I was used to helping very young baby-sitting charges work on learning their colors. I would say, "What color is the apple? What color is the sky?" But I'd never done anything quite like this before.

Soon we'd gone through a whole stack of magazines. I pulled out a couple more from Whitney's huge stack, but she pushed them to one side and shook her head impatiently.

"I'm tired of magazines," she said.

I thought for a moment of the Kid-Kits we use in the BSC back in Connecticut. Kid-Kits (another brilliant Kristy invention) are boxes that we take on some of our baby-sitting jobs. Inside the boxes are books and puzzles and toys, not necessarily new things, but things that are new to the kids we're taking care of.

They're always fascinated by the contents of the Kid-Kits and are delighted to be allowed to play with the "new" stuff inside.

But a Kid-Kit wouldn't work for Whitney. Even if the contents did interest her, she'd probably feel it was too babyish. Also, I didn't want to do anything that might make her think I was baby-sitting for her.

"Do you like to play games?" I asked.

Whitney looked wary. "Sometimes. But at school when we play games, sometimes it means we have to pick up our toys and help clean up the room."

I had to laugh. "Yeah. Don't you hate it when teachers try to trick you like that?"

Whitney nodded emphatically. "They should just say, 'Will you please pick everything up from the floor?' "

I suddenly remembered that Sunny was sitting for Clover and Daffodil Austin, who lived next door to me.

"Hey, Whitney, remember the job I told you about? The one I have baby-sitting as a member of the We Love Kids Club?"

"Yes! Baby-sitting. I want to baby-sit," said Whitney.

"Right. Well, a friend of mine, Sunny, has a baby-sitting job near here too — er — today. Right now, in fact. We could go visit her at work."

Nodding excitedly, Whitney said, "Yes. Let's do that."

Whew! She hadn't noticed my slip-up, when I referred to Sunny having a baby-sitting job, *too*. I stood up and reached down to pull Whitney to her feet. She lost her balance a little and she nearly pulled me over.

"Oops," I said, staggering and regaining my balance.

"Oops," repeated Whitney.

I left a note for Mr. and Mrs. Cater in case they came home early (although I didn't think that they would), and Whitney and I set out for the Austins'.

Since we had another perfect day, complete with all the best colors of summer, from amazing sky blue to sunshine gold, I wasn't surprised when we reached the Austins' to find the girls in their bathing suits, playing with hoses and sprinklers. Clover was clutching a big flower that squirted water and chasing Daffodil through the sprinklers shooting water at her. "I'm raining flowers, I'm raining flowers!" Clover was shouting. Although she was soaking wet like her sister, Daffodil was shrieking every time Clover sprayed her.

Daffodil is nine and Clover is six, but Clover is the Austin you notice first. She lives at the top of her lungs, sort of like Karen, Kristy's little sister. She saw me and shouted, "DAWN!"

Whitney's eyes widened and I laughed. "Hi, Clover! Hi, Daffodil." Daffodil, still running from Clover, waved her arms in what might have been a greeting as Whitney and I strolled over to join Sunny, who was watching from the *extreme* edge of the water fight.

"Sunny," I said. "Hi. This is Whitney. I told her about the We Love Kids Club and she wanted to come with me to visit you while you work."

I'd already told Sunny and the others that my baby-sitting job with Whitney was undercover, so I knew Sunny wouldn't give me away.

Whitney held out her hand. After a moment, Sunny took it and gave it a little shake.

"It is nice to meet you, Sunny," said Whitney, in the same careful, practiced way she'd spoken when she'd met me.

Sunny paused, then said, "I'm glad to meet you, too. Whitney. Want to join Clover and Daffodil?"

"Yes!" exclaimed Whitney instantly.

"Dawn?" said Sunny. *I* knew she was asking me if it was all right for Whitney to join in, but Whitney didn't.

"You'll play, too, won't you, Dawn? You want to?"

I hesitated. As Whitney's "friend" there was no reason for me not to join in the sprinkler frolics, but as the person responsible for her, I didn't know if it was such a good idea.

Fortunately, Sunny came to my rescue. "If Dawn doesn't want to, she could keep me company."

"Okay," said Whitney. "I need my bathing suit." She turned back toward her house.

"Whitney, wait," I said. To Sunny, I said, "See you in a few minutes."

"We'll be here," Sunny assured me.

I had to hurry to keep up with Whitney as she went back home. I changed the note to the Caters, telling them where we were and what we were doing, while Whitney changed into her bathing suit. A few minutes later, she came out wearing a bathing cap, and a big shirt that almost reached her knees. She was carrying a towel and a small plastic container in her hand.

"Shoes?" I said, pointing.

"Oh. Thank you, Dawn. I almost forgot."

She returned a minute later wearing sneakers.

"What have you got in there?" I asked, indicating the plastic container in her left hand.

"Ear plugs," said Whitney. "They're special ear plugs. Water makes my ears hurt sometimes and I have to take medicine. But if I wear these every time I swim, then my ears don't hurt and I don't have to take medicine."

"Ear infections," I said, remembering what Mr. Cater had said.

"That's right," said Whitney, pleased that I had "guessed."

"You have drops, too, to put in before and after?"

Whitney looked at me in surprise and I said, "When you are a baby-sitter, you have to know these things."

"Yes. But I'm not swimming. Do I need the drops?"

"Better safe than sorry," I said. Mrs. Cater had told me the drops were in the downstairs bathroom cabinet. "I'll get them," I said, and hurried away.

Whitney was waiting impatiently when I reached the front porch. "Come *on*, Dawn," she said.

"Coming, coming," I said, laughing.

When we got back to the Austins', Whitney carefully put her ear drops in, then her ear plugs, then folded her towel, lined her sneakers up next to it, gave the ear drops back to me, and slid the ear plug container into the toe of one of the sneakers. Then she turned and waved wildly.

I ducked. "Whoa, Whitney!"

"I'm heeeere," she called to Clover and Daffodil, and waded into the sprinklers.

"Eek!" shrieked Daffodil, who was now holding the hose to keep Clover at bay. She turned and splashed Whitney and Clover with it.

Whitney put her hands over her head as if she were about to dive headfirst into a swimming pool and dove down the spray of water.

"I'm a hose fish!" cried Whitney.

"A hose fish, a hose fish!" screamed Clover, imitating Whitney, and adding her own wiggly side-to-side movements. She "swam" back toward her sister from the other side.

"EEEEEEK!" Daffodil cried again, flinging down the hose and taking off.

Clover grabbed the hose and turned it on Daffodil and Whitney, who charged away, laughing.

If I'd had any worries about how Clover and Daffodil would take to the "new kid," they'd just been washed away.

"Wow," Sunny said. She sat down on the steps and sprawled out to turn her face up to the sun. "Where do they get so much energy?"

"Pretty amazing," I agreed, imitating Sunny's example.

"Flower fish!" cried Whitney, who'd gotten the hose and was holding it straight up in the air. Clover and Daffodil immediately began to twirl around, making fluttery motions with their hands.

"Sunny, come play," panted Clover, twirling up close and spraying us with water.

"Hey, flower fish, you're watering *me!*" said Sunny, laughing.

"Don't you want to play?" asked Clover, still spinning.

"Thank you, but no thanks. I'll keep Dawn company, okay?"

Clover shrugged and spun away.

We sat in the sun watching the dance of the water flowers for most of the afternoon. The three girls couldn't have been happier.

At last Sunny stood up and walked over to the faucets. "Time for a snack!" she called and turned the water off.

The three, soaking wet, splashed around in the puddles for a moment longer, then came tumbling across the lawn in a spray of water.

"Towels over here," I said.

"Dry off all over," Sunny said, "and we'll all go see about something good to eat."

The kitchen yielded plenty of great food: vegetable chips and yogurt dip, oatmeal raisin cookies, and a slice of watermelon. More than enough food for all of us, even those of us with a huge appetite from lawn swimming, right?

Wrong. Clover and Daffodil both took one look at the watermelon and made a grab for it.

"Mine," said Clover.

"I saw it first," Daffodil said, her voice rising.

"Did not."

"Did too."

"Uh, girls," I said.

"Hey, you two," began Sunny.

Whitney reached out and drew the watermelon back across the table to the middle.

"You should cut the watermelon in half," she said slowly. "You should cut it, Daffodil. Then . . . then Clover gets to pick first. That is fair." She nodded emphatically.

I looked at Sunny. Sunny looked at me. We both looked at the two sisters.

Watermelon fight averted.

"Okay," said Daffodil, picking up the knife. She cut the watermelon very, very carefully in half, making sure that the pieces were exactly even, while Clover watched closely.

Then, after much consideration, Clover chose one of the two identical pieces of watermelon and the two settled back with their treat.

Whitney reached for the oatmeal raisin cookies and Sunny and I made a nice-sized dent in the vegetable chips (of course).

The afternoon ended peacefully, and two tired but happy girls waved enthusiastically as Whitney and I left.

"Come back soon," called Clover.

"Soonnn," echoed Daffodil.

"That was fun," said Whitney.

"Yeah, it was. You were great with Clover and Daffodil." I had been really, truly impressed with Whitney's skill with the two girls, and with her own responsible behavior in wearing the ear plugs and keeping them in.

Whitney ducked her head a little and nodded, smiling. "They're nice. Sunny is nice. She's a good baby-sitter."

"And a good friend," I said, smiling at the memory of Sunny propped back on her elbows in the sun.

"Is Sunny your best friend?" Whitney asked.

"One of them," I said.

We'd reached the last intersection before Whitney's street. It had gotten much busier with the after-work traffic.

Whitney, who'd been about half a step ahead of me, stopped so abruptly that I ran into her.

"Whitney?" I said.

Whitney stepped sideways. Then stepped forward tentatively. A car whizzed by and slammed on its brakes as the light turned yellow. Whitney leaped back and began to rock nervously from one foot to the other.

I looked both ways. The cars had stopped.

"Come on," I said.

Whitney rocked back and forth. "I don't know," she said. "I don't know."

"Whitney?"

"So many cars," said Whitney. "I don't know."

Whitney suddenly sounded very, very young.

"Whitney," I said gently. "It's okay." I reached for her hand, then realized that she might think I was treating her like a baby. So I slid my arm through hers.

"Let's walk across together, okay?"

Whitney stopped rocking back and forth and some of the panic left her eyes. She looked at me, then at the line of stopped cars.

"O-okay, Dawn."

We stepped off the curb and walked across the street together.

"Red makes the cars stop, and lets the people walk across," said Whitney softly as we got to the other side.

"That's right," I said.

"Yes," said Whitney, her panic now completely forgotten. She smiled at me trustingly.

"Can we go see Clover and Daffodil again soon?"

"Sure," I said. "And we'll have a great afternoon tomorrow, too."

"Okay," said Whitney.

I couldn't help but think, as we went back to Whitney's house, how different she was from anyone I'd ever known — so grown-up in so many ways, and so very young in others.

Then I had to laugh at myself. How different, after all, was that from any of us? It was just that, for Whitney, the grown-up part of her mind could only grow up so much. But for most of the rest of us, we had to keep growing up whether we liked it or not.

CHAPTER 5

Wednesday

Seven kids who get along seem like a lot fewer than seven kids who don't get along, if you know what I mean, Claud.

That's the truth, Stacey. And who can forget how much the Barretts and the Dewits didn't get along? But now they are getting along just greeeattt!

So be prepared, Dawn, we're going to write and tell you all about what great baby-sitters Claudia and I are!

Stacey and Claudia were in charge of seven kids for the evening: the three Barretts — eight-year-old Buddy, five-year-old Suzi, and their baby sister Marnie — and the four DeWitts — eight-year-old Lindsey, six-year-old Taylor, four-year-old Madeleine, and two-year-old Ryan.

Since Mr. Franklin DeWitt, the man Mrs. Barrett has been dating, is a very prompt and organized person, he arrived at the Barretts' front door at the same time Stacey and Claudia did, along with the four kids.

"Hi, guys," said Stacey.

"Allow me," said Franklin, and he reached out and rang the doorbell and then made a sort of bow in Stacey and Claudia's direction. All the DeWitt kids giggled and Franklin grinned, obviously pleased with his little joke. He was clearly in a very good mood.

Mrs. Barrett answered the door and smiled radiantly at Franklin. She is someone who is, well, organizationally different, but she always manages to look pulled together and that night was no exception. If Franklin looked handsome in his suit and tie, Mrs. Barrett looked like a model in her silk dress and gold earrings (one of which she was putting on as she opened the door) and upswept hair.

"There you are," she cried, as if it was all

a huge, wonderful surprise to find Franklin, four kids, and two baby-sitters on her front porch. "Come in, come in."

Ryan suddenly got shy, and sidled into the house.

Stacey bent over and scooped him up. "Why don't I give you a ride for a little while, Ryan? How would you like that?"

Ryan nodded, and Stacey boosted him onto her back while Mrs. Barrett grabbed her purse and gave Stacey and Claudia last minute instructions.

"Dinner is — " said Mrs. Barrett and waved her hand in the direction of the kitchen.

"Potluck?" supplied Franklin, smiling. "A smorgasbord? Everything sandwiches?"

"Exactly!" Mrs. Barrett beamed at him and seemed to forget that anyone else was standing in the hall except Franklin and her.

Claudia cleared her throat. "Great. Um, approximately what time will you . . ."

"Early," said Franklin, smiling at Mrs. Barrett the same way. "No later than eight. It's just a cocktail party. A business thing, really."

"Great," said Claudia again.

No one moved for a moment. Then Stacey said, "So, Mrs. Barrett, Mr. DeWitt, have a good time."

That broke the spell, at least for the moment.

Mrs. Barrett, her cheeks a little pink, nodded and said, "Thank you."

"We will," said Franklin, still looking at Mrs. Barrett. He made the same sort of funny little bow he'd made on the porch but no one giggled. When he held out his arm, Mrs. Barrett took it and sort of floated out the door with him.

"What's a smorgasbord?" asked Lindsey DeWitt. "Is it good?"

"Well, it's sort of potluck, I guess," said Claudia.

"What's a potluck?" asked Suzi.

"That's when the guests who go to a party each bring a special dish. That's a potluck supper."

"Oh," said Suzi.

"A smorgasbord is more like all kinds of different foods that people can pick and choose to eat from. Like you put it out on a table and . . ."

"A cafeteria!" exclaimed Buddy.

"Sort of like that, too," said Stacey. "Only I think you can go back as many times as you want and get all kinds of different things."

"Can we have smorgas . . . smorgas . . . potluck?" asked Taylor DeWitt.

Stacey thought for a moment. It was a beautiful summer evening, clear and not too warm.

"It would be nice to do something outside," she said.

"What about a smorgasbord picnic?" suggested Claudia. "We'll put everything out on the table here and fix a picnic from it and then take it to the park and play games and have a picnic. A smorgaspic!"

"A smorgaspic!" cried Taylor.

Marnie Barrett clapped her hands together.

Soon the seven kids were running back and forth in the kitchen, lining things up on the kitchen table.

"Ketchup, pickles, tuna salad," chanted Buddy, leaning forward to look in the refrigerator.

"Hand off!" said Lindsey behind him and Bryan reached in and grabbed the ketchup and the pickles and the tuna salad, one at a time, and passed them back to Lindsey, who set them on the table.

"Bread," cried Taylor as he emerged from the pantry, holding a loaf of whole wheat bread aloft.

"Baloney, jelly, and stinky cheese," Buddy went on.

"Euuww, stinky cheese!" shouted Suzi. She took the package, labeled *gorgonzola*, out of Lindsey's hand and sniffed it, then frowned. "It doesn't stink."

Lindsey laughed and peeled back a corner of the wrapper. "Now smell," she said.

Suzi leaned over and sniffed again, then shrieked delightedly, "Euuw, euuw, stinky, stinky!"

"Stinky!" cried Marnie, joining in the excitement.

"Inky," whispered Ryan, who'd been dropping the napkins one by one into a basket Claudia had given him.

When the table couldn't hold any more food, the seven kids set to work making a smorgaspic, with a little help from Claudia and Stacey.

They loaded the picnic into Suzi's wagon and took turns pulling the wagon to the park, with Suzi and Taylor pulling the wagon together for their turn.

It was hard to believe this was the same group of kids that once got along so badly they had to be separated when people baby-sat for them together. That had been back when they first met, right after Mrs. Barrett and Franklin had started going out. But once they got used to the idea of their respective parents seeing each other, and once Mrs. Barrett and Mr. DeWitt stopped trying so hard to make everybody like everybody, and just let people be themselves (with a little help from the members of the BSC, world-class baby-sitters), the seven kids now got along okay.

They even seemed to share the same bizarre taste in food, as Stacey and Claudia discovered at the park.

After a killer game of freeze tag and a very funny game of pass the egg on the spoon (Stacey had snagged a couple of hard-boiled eggs from the refrigerator, which were completely cracked and mushed by the time the game was over), the smorgaspic got underway.

Stacey had packed an apple and a container of leftover rice and black beans, because she has to be careful about what she eats. It was a good thing she had, because the smorgaspic had a truly stunning assortment of food. It even stunned Claudia, who picked up what she thought was a tuna salad sandwich and took a big bite.

"W-what is this!" she gasped, making a hideous face.

"Claudia?" asked Stacey. "Are you all right?"

Claudia peeled the top of the sandwich back while the Barretts and the DeWitts burst into laughter. "Oreos!" cried Claudia. "Who put crushed Oreos on my sandwich?"

Taylor reached out and took the sandwich. "I invented it," he said. "Like that Ben & Jerry's ice cream."

56

"Chocolate chip Oreo Crunch this is *not*," said Claudia.

Taylor took a big bite and said, "I like it."

"Can I try it?" asked Suzi. She took a bite, chewed thoughtfully for a minute, then said, "I like it, too."

Claudia fished around and found a plain tuna sandwich. But among the sandwiches she and Stacey watched the Barretts and the DeWitts eat and share with each other with gusto, in addition to the tuna salad and Oreo, were a peanut butter and potato chip, a cole slaw and baloney, and a grape jelly and cheddar cheese.

As they trudged home from the park, full and tired, Stacey said, "I hope they don't have stomachaches."

Claudia shuddered. "I thought I was a junk food fanatic, but this group has got me beat. Still, your food just gets all mixed together in your stomach anyway."

"Thanks for sharing that, Claudia," said Stacey, making a face of her own.

After all the games and the smorgaspic, Marnie went easily to bed, and since Ryan was looking a little sleepy himself, they tucked him into Buddy's bed.

Then they took turns reading an old book that Buddy had found on one of the bookshelves: *Cheaper By the Dozen*, about a family with twelve kids in it. It was sort of old-fashioned, but it was funny, too.

Not too long after that, Mrs. Barrett and Franklin returned. Mrs. Barrett was holding onto Franklin's arm just as she had been when they left. And she was still staring at him in that same mesmerized way, only her cheeks were very pink. She was practically glowing, and so was Franklin.

"Was it fun?" asked Claudia, as Mrs. Barrett was paying them.

"What? Oh, the party. Oh, it was *wonderful*," breathed Mrs. Barrett. The two adults exchanged a long look.

Franklin said, "Truly wonderful. The most special night of my life."

"Oh. Well, great," said Stacey. She grabbed Claudia's elbow and steered her out the door.

"I wonder what's going on?" said Claudia.

"I don't know, but something's up," said Stacey. "Oh, well, at least the days of the Barrett/DeWitt feud are over."

"Forever," agreed Claudia.

"And ever," said Stacey.

CHAPTER 6

"Hello, hello, hel-lo!" My father bounded through the door of the den.

I looked at him. He was smiling. Was this a good sign or a bad sign? He was just coming in from another one of his first dates. "Clarice Dubina" he'd said over his shoulder as he'd rushed out to his date earlier in the evening. "More later."

I guess later had arrived. I pointed the remote toward the television and clicked it off.

"Hi, Dad," I said. "What's up?"

"Why did the lobster move to a bigger house?" asked my father.

"Is this a Jeff joke?" I asked.

Jeff, who was sprawled on the floor, shook his head. "Nope," he said.

"You'll like it, Jeff. Go on, why did the lobster move to a bigger house."

"I give up," I said immediately. "Why?"

Jeff took longer. His professional reputation

as a comedian was at stake. But at last he said, too, "I give up."

"Because he had 'clawstrophobia'! Get it? Claustrophobia."

I managed to smile. "I get it, Dad."

Jeff gave a big horse laugh. "That's great, Dad! Where did you hear that one?"

"Our waiter at the restaurant tonight."

I had a sudden flash of inspiration. "Did you go to the Ocean Inn for dinner?" The Ocean Inn was a local seafood house, really plain inside, but heaps of seafood on every plate.

And waiters who were planning to be comedians, obviously.

Dad nodded and beamed as if I'd gotten the right answer on a game show. "It was great," he said. "Terrific. I like someone who can match me oyster for oyster."

"You ate *raw* oysters?" Jeff grabbed his throat and let his head drop to one side.

"Yup. Wait and see, Jeff. You'll try them someday and like them, too."

I didn't want to clutch my throat and act like Jeff, but I admit, the idea of *ever* letting a slimy, raw oyster touch my lips made me go "ick" inside. But I smiled and said (bravely), "Sounds like fun, Dad."

"It was. It definitely was. So . . ."

"Time for the family date," I finished.

Dad nodded. "A carnival is scheduled to roll into town this weekend. Clarice thought it might be a fun outing for all of us."

"A carnival?" Jeff recovered from his imaginary oyster wipeout to sit up and protest. "That's for little kids!" But from the sparkle in his eyes, I could tell he was hooked on the idea.

"Little kids!" My father pretended to be indignant. "I'm not a little kid and I love carnivals. The rides, the games, the cotton candy . . ."

"The popcorn," I put in quickly. (Ugh! Oysters and cotton candy in one conversation.) "The people. I like carnivals too, Dad."

"Well," Jeff said. "Okay. If you two really want to go, I guess I could come, too."

"Great," said my father. "Saturday carnival it is. This is going to be *fun*."

Did I mention that my father is one of those weird eternal optimists?

The carnival was a disaster.

We picked up Clarice and my heart sank when she slid into the car, turned to look at Jeff and me sitting in the back seat, and said, "So these are the children. They're a great looking pair, Schaf."

Schaf? *Schaf*? Jeff and I exchanged glances, but then I thought, hey, what's in a nickname? Look at mine.

"Hi," I said, deciding to ignore the nickname and the fact that she'd just called me and Jeff children. "I'm Dawn and this is Jeff."

Jeff didn't say anything. I elbowed him. Hard.

"Owww," cried Jeff.

"Now children, no fighting. We'll be there in just a few minutes, won't we, Schaf?" Clarice gave us a big, big smile and turned back to my father.

Children. She'd done it again. Beside me, Jeff folded his arms. I didn't have to look at him to know that his eyes were narrow and his lower lip was sticking out. He had jumped, hyper-speed, into one of his ornery moods. It didn't bode well for the evening.

I was right.

Bright lights, lots of noise, the smell of popcorn and cotton candy, the grind of the motors, and the shrieks of the people on the rides, the clanging of bells and whistles and sirens at all the games, enormous silly stuffed animals — the carnival had everything it was supposed to have.

Except three Schafers and one Clarice having a good time.

Clarice started talking the moment we hit the midway and she didn't stop the whole time, pointing things out to us, grabbing our arms and squeezing our shoulders for emphasis, telling Schaf that the children would love this ride or that.

"Look," she exclaimed. She squeezed my father's arm, my shoulder, and ruffled Jeff's hair before he could duck out of the way. "Bumper cars!"

"Boring," said Jeff.

"Silly boy!" cried Clarice. "Come on, Schaf, let's show the children we old people can still do the bump!" Clarice charged up to the ticket booth with our father in tow and a few minutes later we were seated in our respective bumper cars.

I looked over at Jeff. He was looking at Clarice. It didn't take a rocket scientist to figure out what would happen next.

Wham! Jeff plowed into the side of Clarice's bumper car.

She gave a little shriek of laughter and began to frantically turn her wheel. But Jeff didn't give her a chance. "Wham! Wham!" Clarice's car spun round and round. "Wham!"

Clarice's mouth opened, but before she could laugh, Jeff got her again.

Whack! Someone jolted into me and I lost sight of the two, and spent the rest of the time maintaining my own bumper car defense. But I was pretty sure that no one attacked me as relentlessly as Jeff attacked Clarice.

I had to give Clarice credit, though. She

smiled brightly as we climbed out of our cars, and said, as if she hadn't even noticed Jeff's all out attack, "Now, wasn't that fun?"

"Terrific," said Jeff. "Let's do it again."

"Not now, Jeff," said our father quickly. Dad had noticed even if Clarice hadn't.

Jeff accepted that easily. Too easily. The next minute he was pointing at a booth where giant lime green pandas dangled from the rafters. "Look, Dawn! You remember how you've always tried and tried to win one of those? Let's go try again!"

"*What?*" Before I could protest or say Jeff was crazy, Clarice had said, "Oh, Dawn, really? Well, let's see what we can do about getting you the toy of your dreams."

"Toy?" I said. "But . . ."

Too late. Clarice had already marched over to the booth and plunked down her money for three balls to knock over a stack of three pins.

She missed.

She missed again.

"That's okay," I said. "Really."

"No, no, no," said Clarice.

I resigned myself to wandering the carnival for the rest of the night lugging a green panda. Maybe I could give it to Whitney, I thought. Or to Clover or Daffodil.

Unfortunately, Clarice's aim was terrible. She tried and tried and tried, but she couldn't win. And Jeff, the little rat, kept encouraging her, looking over his shoulder to say things like, "Don't worry, Dawn. She'll get it this time."

Finally my father cleared his throat. "Tell you what, next time I see a panda in the store, I'll buy you one, Dawn."

Just at that moment, Clarice succeeded. "Ha!" she cried. "There, Schaf." She seized the panda from the grinning booth operator and bestowed it on me.

"Thanks," I said weakly. I was going to get Jeff for this!

"No problem, kiddo," Clarice said.

"Time for — " our father began.

"Cotton candy! I haven't had that in years. Since I was a child," Clarice said. "I remember I used to make myself positively *sick* on cotton candy. Do you children do that?"

"How about popcorn, Dad?" I said quickly, as my father stopped one of the vendors.

"What a *good* girl you are," gushed Clarice. "But I'm going to have cotton candy." So did Dad, to be polite, I guess. But Jeff and I stuck to popcorn. We weren't ready to go into polite sugar overload for anyone.

Two cotton candies and two popcorns later,

we stopped at the end of the midway. My father looked at his watch. "Well, time to go," he said.

"Oh, Schaf, really. I was having such fun," said Clarice.

"Aw, Dad," said Jeff.

I frowned suspiciously at Jeff. What was he up to now?

Jeff pointed at the Scrambler. "Couldn't we just ride on that?"

"Let's all ride it!" said Clarice, clapping her hands.

I winced. "No thanks," I said. "It's too wild for me."

"Chicken," said Jeff.

My father said, "I hate to say it, but it's probably too much for me, too."

"Aww," said Jeff. "It's no fun alone."

Clarice took the bait. "I'll ride it with you, Jeff. Schaf, you and Dawn don't mind waiting here, do you?"

"No problem," said my father.

But it was a problem. Poor Clarice staggered off the Scrambler and into the nearest restroom and was sick.

"Gosh," said Jeff. "I didn't know she was going to *barf*."

My father said, "That will be enough, Jeff." Jeff must have realized he was pushing his luck, because he didn't say anything else, not even when Clarice emerged, looking a bit wan.

"Are you all right? Is there anything I can do?" my father asked.

"I'll be fine," said Clarice. "Just give me a minute."

Poor Clarice. She must have felt awful. She was quiet all the way to the car and almost all the way home. I was actually feeling sorry for her — until, as we passed the mall, she sat up and said, "You know, Dawn, we should go shopping together."

"Uh, sure," I said.

"And soon," Clarice went on. "For those things that just us girls can shop for."

"Uh . . ." I said.

"Schaf, I don't know what you were thinking of, letting Dawn go buy a bra on her own. It clearly isn't the proper fit. You need a woman's touch for that sort of thing."

I was *mortified*.

"Oooh, Dawn," said Jeff. I gave him such a fierce glare that he stopped. "Oh. Sorry," he muttered.

My father said, "Dawn's grown-up enough to handle quite a few things herself. I think this is one of them. . . . Here we are."

He pulled the car over to the curb and got out to walk Clarice to her door. When he came back, I said, "Dad?"

My father started the car and said, "I know,

I know." He sighed. "Too bad things didn't work out. She's a nice person but . . ."

This dating stuff was wearing me out. I didn't see how my father kept it up.

I did mention that he was an eternal optimist, though, didn't I?

Exactly nine days later we were out on another family date.

Barbara Hinkley. My father had met her at the dentist's office, which should have been a clue. That and the fact that she showed up for the date — to Cap'n Frank's Fun Fish Fry, where the waiters and waitresses are dressed like buccaneers, the food is served in plastic pirate ships, and the dishes all have cute little nautical names — wearing a suit.

Don't get me wrong. It was a great looking suit, a pinstripe with a long jacket. She was wearing a beautiful silk wrap blouse under it, gorgeous gold earrings, and carrying a soft leather clutch purse that matched her heels.

My father was wearing chinos, a Polo shirt, and a windbreaker. Jeff and I were in nice jeans with cotton sweaters and sneakers.

My father seemed disconcerted when she walked through the door of the restaurant (she'd told him she preferred to meet us there) and surveyed the room.

Barbara looked downright disapproving as she walked up to the table and sat down. But all she said was, "What an interesting place, Richard," in a cool, polite voice that said, NOT.

The evening went downhill after that.

"I'll have the Shiver Me Timbers Platter," Jeff said, "with double fries . . ."

"Double fries? That's a fried seafood *platter*, Jeffrey. Surely you're getting enough. You don't want to waste food." Barbara's tone was totally disapproving.

"Dad?" Jeff appealed to our father, who was sitting there looking uncomfortable.

"Jeff can handle it if anybody can, Barbara, believe me," Dad said.

"Double fries," repeated Jeff triumphantly, "And the Whale of a Soft Drink-size coke."

I got the Schooner Sandwich (with broiled clams) and a green salad (the SeaGreen Delight), which was the healthiest thing I could find on the menu.

Dad got the Deep Six Claws Platter (crab and lobster).

Barbara said, "I'll have plain broiled fish, lemon on the side, a small green salad, oil and vinegar dressing on the side, and a seltzer with lime."

The waitress, who was wearing a pirate hat said, "The Shoreline Special."

"No," corrected Barbara. "I don't want french fries. I don't want slaw. I don't want

69

your special sea sauce, whatever that is. *Plain* broiled fish, lemon on the side, a small green salad, oil and vinegar dressing on the side, and a seltzer with lime. Period. And, young lady? I will send it back if it is not as I asked for it."

"Oh!" The waitress's cheeks got pink, but she wrote it all down and said, "Certainly. Anything else?"

That was it. For the entire evening. If you don't count Barbara correcting Jeff and me on our table manners, commenting on what we were eating, trying to prevent Jeff from ordering dessert, urging me to drink some milk because it was especially important for adolescents to get enough calcium, and generally being picky and uptight.

By the time the meal was over, I would have been glad to make her walk the plank. And I was as glad as I've ever been to see her shake my father's hand, say, "Well, it's been an interesting experience," and walk away.

My father stood there for a moment, watching. Then he turned. "Oh, well," he said. "Can't win them all, can you, guys?"

"It's okay, Dad," said Jeff. "The food was great!"

CHAPTER 7

"So long, Dad!" shouted Whitney cheerfully.

Mr. Cater made a face, then smiled. "You sound like you're glad to see me go," he teased gently.

Whitney gave a snort of laughter and threw her arms around her father so hard he rocked backward. "No," she said, giving him a huge bear hug. "But Dawn came to visit." She suddenly straightened up and said very formally, "We will see you later."

"Okay. 'Bye, Whitney, Dawn."

"Good-bye," said Whitney.

" 'Bye, Mr. Cater," I said.

We listened as Whitney's father's footsteps crossed the hall. A moment later the front door closed.

"Too bad people have to work," I said, looking out of Whitney's bedroom window at the bright sunshine. "It's such a great day."

"Great," Whitney echoed.

I looked around the room. Through the half open door of Whitney's closet I caught a glimpse of familiar lime-green. It looked like the green panda that Clarice had won for me on the disastrous family date to the carnival. I'd given it to Whitney and she had put it proudly on the chair in her room and named it Buster.

"Is that Buster in the closet?" I asked.

Whitney nodded without looking toward Buster.

"Why?"

Her eyebrows snapping together in a frown, Whitney said, "Because Buster is for babies. I'm too grown-up for him now."

"Oh." Surveying the room, I realized that all of Whitney's dolls and stuffed animals had disappeared — into the closet, I suspected. "I see. Well, so, what do you want to do today?"

Whitney's frown stayed in place. "Something grown-up," she replied. "I want to go to the mall." She sounded as if she expected me to disagree with her. I wondered briefly if it was something that was a special treat for Whitney, or something that her parents didn't do at all. But I couldn't imagine why, nor had they mentioned anything about it.

"Well, we can't go to the big mall because it's too far," I said. Whitney frowned harder.

I went on, "But we can walk to the one near here. That'd be great." I watched the frown disappear from Whitney's face as if by magic.

"Great!" she echoed, and made a dive for the piggy bank sitting on her dresser. She emptied it out on her bed, then pulled a large old leather shoulder purse from the top shelf of her closet.

"My mom gave me this," she explained. "It's a grown-up purse, see? It has a zipper pouch inside and its own matching coin purse."

Whitney crammed the money from the bed into the change purse, then stuck the change purse into the zipper compartment.

"Ready?" I asked.

"Yes," said Whitney excitedly.

"Then let's go."

The mall wasn't far away at all and the walk through Whitney's neighborhood was a pleasant one. When we reached the big intersection to cross to the mall, I remembered how flustered Whitney had gotten once before at an intersection, so I linked my arm through hers as we waited for the light to change. "We're almost there," I said.

Whitney nodded. When we reached the other side, I slipped my arm free of Whitney's and pretended to adjust my backpack so Whitney wouldn't think I had been treating her like a baby, leading her across the street.

But Whitney's eyes were focused on Hudson's department store ahead. She kept snapping and unsnapping the clasp on the purse.

"Ready, set, spend," I joked as we reached the walk outside the mall. Whitney just nodded again.

We went to Hudson's. The first things we saw as we walked in the door were the makeup and perfume counters. Whitney made a beeline for them.

She picked up a sampler bottle. "Pretty," she said. "What's this?"

I looked at the label. "Poison," I read aloud.

Whitney's eyes widened and she set the bottle down quickly.

"No, no, Whitney. It's not really poison. That's the name of the perfume, see?" I picked up the bottle, turned Whitney's wrist over and sprayed a little on it.

Whitney sniffed her wrist, then wrinkled her nose. I sniffed it, too, and had to agree.

"It's strong," I said. "Phew."

We walked from counter to counter, smelling the different perfumes.

"Look," said Whitney. She pointed to the Chanel counter. "That's what my mother wears."

"Chanel?" I said. "Very classy." We walked over and I picked up the sampler bottle. "Wait a minute, Whitney! You're out of wrists. You'll have to put some on my wrist."

I was about to hand the bottle to Whitney when a frosty voice said, "May I help you?"

I turned my head and saw a thin woman with frosted hair and a ton of blush on her cheeks staring at us. Her eyes went from me to Whitney's and widened. She stared at Whitney and I felt a flush of annoyance. She was so rude!

"We're sampling the perfumes," I said in my most grown-up voice.

Without warning, the woman grabbed the bottle from my hand. "Here, I'll do that." She sprayed a tiny amount on my wrist, then said, her voice even colder, "Will there be anything else?"

Whitney looked puzzled.

"No, thank you," I said, making my voice as frosty as hers. "We've had quite enough of your help. Come on, Whitney."

I turned and stomped away.

"Dawn?"

"Sorry, Whitney. She made me mad. I guess . . . I guess she doesn't like her job."

Whitney accepted that. "Can I smell your wrist?" She bent over and sniffed. "My mother's perfume!" she exclaimed in a loud voice. A pair of women standing at a nearby discount makeup table turned and stared. One leaned over and whispered something into the other's ear.

I knew they were talking about Whitney. I glared at them and they saw me and turned quickly away.

Good grief. How could people be so rude? It isn't as if Down's syndrome is all that uncommon. Hadn't people ever seen anyone like Whitney before? Hadn't they ever seen anyone who was a little different?

I had told Whitney how some companies test makeup on animals and hurt them, but I didn't think she'd remembered. However, I realized she had when we next stopped by a makeup counter (where the sales clerk didn't, for a change, stare at Whitney or act as if Whitney might do something weird). She just smiled and said, "The newest in this line of lipsticks. I'm wearing that color. Do you girls want to see anything?"

Whitney said, "Do you do things to animals with those?"

The clerk looked surprised for a moment, then said, "Oh, you mean animal testing. No, we don't do animal testing with any of our products, including the perfume."

"Good," said Whitney. With the clerk's help, she tried two of the lipsticks on the back of her hand. "Pretty," she said.

The clerk nodded. "It wears well, too. It will last a long, long time."

I bought some lotion with a sunscreen in it and before we left, the clerk reached under the counter and pulled out two tiny vials attached to cards. "Here's a sample of our perfume for you," she said. "Oceanambre. I think you'll like it."

"Thanks!" I said.

Whitney beamed. "Thank you very much," she said in her best grown-up voice.

People weren't so bad, after all, I was deciding as we walked out of the store. I lifted my face to the sun coming through the skylights above and was feeling pretty good as we walked beneath the potted palms. But it was too soon to relax, as I quickly discovered.

At least half the people we passed stared at Whitney. A lot of them whispered to one another or giggled or both. It was disgusting.

"Look!" cried Whitney.

People turned, people stared, people giggled and whispered. How could Whitney not notice? Didn't it hurt her?

But she didn't seem to associate the reactions of those around her with herself. She pointed at the hair-bead store and practically dragged me in.

Now it was Whitney's turn to stare. The

proprietor of the store had dozens and dozens of beaded braids of hair all over her head. They made a clicking sound when she moved. It was really spectacular.

"Ohhh," breathed Whitney. She pointed. "I want my hair to look like that."

"Don't point, Whitney. It's rude," I whispered automatically, as if she were one of my regular baby-sitting charges. Oops.

But she lowered her arm obediently and the proprietor smiled.

"It took me a long time to get my hair this way, sugar," she said. "And you need good strong hair to do it. Yours might be a little thin for that. But come on over here and let's see what we can do."

After much 'deliberation, Whitney picked out a set of beads and the proprietor wove them into a strand of her hair. Whitney examined herself in the mirror and said, "It's beautiful. Isn't it beautiful, Dawn?"

"It sure is, Whitney," I said.

The proprietor nodded. "They'll all slip off if you undo the bottom part of the strand, here," she explained. "But you can keep them in while you wash your hair if you want. Some beads you can't, of course, but these you can."

Opening her purse, Whitney carefully counted out her money.

"Thank you," she said as we left.

"My pleasure," said the proprietor. "Come back soon."

From the bead store, Whitney zoomed into the earring store. She immediately wanted to get her ears pierced.

"No," I said flatly.

"Why not? You have yours pierced, Dawn. I want my ears to be pierced, too."

"Whitney, I had to get my parents' permission to do this. I tell you what. If your parents agree that you can get your ears pierced, we'll come back and do it, okay?"

Whitney sighed, but she said, "Okay."

"Meanwhile, what about some stick-on earrings?" I asked.

Bending forward, Whitney peered at the sheet of stick-on earrings to which I was pointing.

Suddenly the woman beside us turned. She stared at Whitney, then jerked away so quickly she bumped into the counter behind her. Then she began to back up, still staring.

Staring at Whitney. Acting as if Whitney had some kind of contagious disease, or was dirty or something.

Beside me, Whitney said, "I want these," and opened her purse. She never seemed to notice.

After she bought the earrings, Whitney stuck a pair of red flowers on her earlobes.

Then we went to try on hats with her new look: big hats, silly hats, baseball caps. It was a lot of fun.

Or it would have been, if I hadn't been so aware now of how awful people were acting. At last I couldn't take it anymore. I had had enough.

I took off a big straw hat with a giant flower and put it back on the hat stand. "Time to go, Whitney," I said, trying to make my voice cheerful and unconcerned.

"Really?" Reluctantly, Whitney took off a sequined baseball cap and put it back.

We walked out into the mall and headed toward the exit. At the last minute, Whitney veered away.

"Whitney," I began.

"Just one more store, Dawn, okay? Please?"

"Well . . ."

"Please, please, please?"

I couldn't help but smile. "Okay."

Whitney grabbed my arm. "By myself. I want to do this by myself."

Seeing my objection in my face, she hurried on, "I'll just go right there. You can wait here for me." She pointed at a store that had a neon "Wild Things" sign above the entrance. Through the glass I could see stacks of multicolored socks, shelves of troll dolls, and a conglomeration of miscellany.

"Okay," I said.

Whitney thrust the bag holding the sheet of earrings into my hands then hurried off, her arms swinging and the purse whirling by her side. She looked happy and excited.

At least to me. I wondered what she looked like to all the rude people who whispered and stared as she rushed by.

A few minutes later, Whitney emerged clutching a shopping bag. "Here," she said.

I opened the bag and Whitney reached inside and pulled out a Best Friends necklace. Carefully, ceremoniously, she gave me half.

"Because you are my best friend," Whitney said, looking intently at me, her cheeks pink. "My best friend in the whole world."

I looked down at the necklace, then back at Whitney.

Whitney had started out as a job. But she had become a friend, too.

"Oh, Whitney, thank you," I said softly. "I'll keep this forever."

And I knew that I would.

CHAPTER 8

"Dawn, Jeff, I'm glad to meet you."

Karina Whitaker held out her hand and shook our hands.

"Hey!" said Jeff, and I could tell he was impressed.

"I'm glad to meet you, too," I said, and this time thought that maybe I meant it.

We were about to go out on another one of our family dates with our father. But Karina actually seemed nice and normal: not too formal, not too loud, not too anything else.

"Well, then, let's go," said my father, looking pleased. "The wonderful world of performances *al fresco* waits for no man. Or woman."

Performances *al fresco* meant performances outside. We were going to an outdoor band concert, classical music but cool-sounding classical music, with lots of special effects and neat-looking musicians. At least I thought they were neat-looking when we got there.

I thought the crowd looked pretty cool, too. Lots of families with their baby-sitting charges, er, I mean their children, and an incredible variety of picnic baskets and chairs and blankets and food smells. We got there early to get a good seat and we did, close enough to watch the band (or maybe I mean orchestra) set up, but far enough away so we weren't right in the middle of a gazillion people.

Of course, Jeff spotted somebody he knew immediately and zoomed off after swiping a granola bar out of the basket. Dad and Karina and I laughed and began to spread out the blanket and the picnic.

It was a pretty great picnic, if I do say so myself. I'd helped Mrs. B prepare it, and I enjoyed listening to Karina and my father ooh and ah as I took out tiny cherry tomatoes stuffed with spicy cheese filling; avocado, spinach, and red onion sandwiches with walnut oil vinaigrette on seven grain bread; mozzarella sandwiches with roasted red peppers and pickled mushrooms on Italian bread; peanut butter and apple butter sandwiches on whole wheat bread; new potato salad with dill; and grapes and strawberries and kiwi fruit salad with poppy seed dressing. Plus granola bars for snacks.

"And for dessert we have cheesecake with raspberry sauce," I announced, taking the last bottle of sparkling water out of the cooler.

"This is *amazing*, Dawn," said Karina. "You must have worked for *hours*."

"Healthy and delicious-looking," said my father. "Thank you, Dawn."

"Anytime," I said airily, but I was pleased. Then I saw Sunny and her family nearby. Sunny hadn't seen us yet, so I jumped up. "I'm going to go say hello to Sunny," I told Dad. "I'll be right back."

Sunny didn't see me until I was right behind her and tapped her on the shoulder. She turned and I realized she was wearing her radio headset.

"Dawn!" she cried in a voice that you could hear all the way to the ocean.

I winced and put my hands over my ears and pointed to the headphones.

Sunny reached up, took them off, and grinned. "Sorry," she said in a normal tone of voice.

"This is supposed to be a concert," I said.

"Yeah, but what if I don't like the music?" Sunny asked. "A good baby-sitter is always prepared."

"True," I said. "But I think this is going to be kind of cool. Look, there are the Austins."

We turned and waved at the girls, then surveyed the crowd. The slope in front of the park bandshell was filling up fast.

"Look at that," said Sunny. "Someone brought a whole sound system practically. You'd think they could go without music until the concert started!"

"Very prepared," I said. "Or something!"

We watched people and did the gossip thing until the musicians finished tuning up. Then I headed back to Dad and Karina. Jeff joined us a minute later and we sat down and began to load our plates.

I speared a tomato and gave the sky (still blue, but turning dark with a few stars appearing) an approving glance, and a figure plunked down on the blanket next to me.

"Dawn!" said Whitney happily. "You're wearing your friendship necklace, just like me."

"Whitney, hey! Of course I am," I said softly. "I didn't see you."

"We just got here," said Whitney. She turned and pointed behind her and I saw the Caters sitting a little ways away. I waved and they waved back and Mrs. Cater, who'd been leaning slightly forward, leaned back and seemed to relax.

"What're you eating? It looks good," said Whitney.

"Didn't you bring a picnic?"

Whitney shook her head regretfully. "We had dinner at home."

"Here," I said, and fixed Whitney a sort of sampler plate with just a little of everything.

"Karina, could you hand me the lemon salt?" I asked, pouring Whitney some soda.

Karina didn't answer. "Karina?" I handed Whitney the soda and looked over at Karina.

Karina was looking at Whitney. With a sinking heart, I saw that the expression on her face was a familiar one: repulsion. And embarrassment.

Hoping I was wrong (after all, it was getting dark), I tried again. "Karina? The lemon salt?"

Karina looked away.

I reached over and got the lemon salt myself.

"MMMMM, this is good, Dawn," said Whitney.

"Cherry tomatoes with spicy cheese filling," I said. "It's sort of a variation on a recipe I had in this great vegetarian restaurant once."

"A vegetable restaurant?" asked Whitney.

Beside me, Jeff nodded. "That's exactly what it is," he said. "No hot dogs. No hamburgers."

I laughed. "Not exactly," I said. "But it's true they don't serve meat."

"Well, you could open a vegetarian restaurant anytime with this meal," said Dad.

Karina remained rigidly silent beside him, her eyes down on her plate, picking at her food.

One of the musicians leaned forward and

grabbed the mike. It made that horrible microphone sound and then he said, "Attention ladies and gentlemen . . ."

"Perfect timing," said my father. "Dessert is cheesecake *and* music."

"Cheesecake. I love cheesecake," said Whitney happily.

Karina, not quite looking at Whitney, said, "I think it is time you went back and joined your parents."

"That's okay," said Whitney. "They said I could stay if it was all right with Dawn."

"Great," I said firmly. "I think you'll like the cheesecake."

I cut cheesecake for Whitney, Dad, Jeff, and me. But not for Karina because when I got to her she said, "I couldn't possibly."

"I ate a lot, too," said Dad. "Wait a little while. You'll have room. We'll save you a piece, won't we, Sunshine?"

Poor Dad. I could tell he'd noticed Karina's behavior, too. Now he was all nervous and jolly, trying to make things okay.

Karina's next remark didn't help. "It's not that I'm full. It's just that the scenery has made me lose me appetite."

My father frowned. My mouth dropped open. Jeff, of course, kept on eating. And fortunately, Whitney didn't seem to hear. Or if she did, she didn't understand.

"This is good, Dawn," she said.

"I'm glad you like it," I managed to answer. "Listen, the music is about to begin."

I'd been right about thinking the music would be cool. It was. The musicians explained a little about each piece, played some variations on the opening bars of each one so we could see what it might have sounded like at the time it was written, then launched into their own cool, funky versions of the classical pieces by guys like Bach and Mozart.

"I like this," said Whitney beside me. As the band launched into another piece, she stood up and began to try to dance, throwing her hands out and making up a song to go with the music. She sang loudly. Of course people turned to look, but Whitney kept on dancing and singing happily, not seeming to notice.

Okay, it wasn't the most appropriate thing to do at a concert. But it wasn't as if it were a formal performance in Carnegie Hall or something, either. And at least Whitney was really enjoying the music, not just nodding off like some of the people around me. I reached up and caught Whitney's arm and said, "Sounds good, Whitney, but I think some people want to listen to the music without the words."

"Oh, okay," said Whitney cheerfully. She

sat back down and turned her face toward the stage, and watched and listened intently all the way through to the end of the piece.

Karina said, softly but clearly, "That was disgusting."

Had Whitney heard? No. I gave Karina the meanest look I could, then grabbed Whitney's hand, stood up, and pulled her to her feet. "Come on, let's go back to your parents."

We walked to them and Whitney said, "Dawn had a picnic. I had a picnic, too."

"Not too much," I said. "A sample picnic. Whitney said you guys had dinner already."

Mrs. Cater smiled and said, "Great. Come on Whitney, sit here by me." Whitney sat down and I said, "Do you mind if I join you for awhile?"

"Not at all," said Mr. Cater. The Caters made room for me on their blanket and I stayed with them for the rest of the concert. I knew it was rude of me not to join Dad and Jeff and Karina, but I didn't care.

I didn't care if I never saw Karina again. I couldn't believe how rude and insensitive and totally obnoxious she had been about Whitney.

What a big loser Karina was. Mentally, I drew a big, black X through her name on Dad's date list.

CHAPTER 9

Saturday

What is that saying? All is fair in love and war? Well, love and war have broken out at the Barretts. Mrs. Barrett and Mr. DeWitt are getting married and that means two happy adults and seven very cranky kids. I tried to tell them about my combined family, and yours, Kristy, but they weren't interested.

Mary Anne had a two-part job on Saturday afternoon: stay with the three Barretts while Mrs. Barrett ran errands, then stay with Mrs. Barrett and help her get dinner ready for Franklin and his four children. It was an unusual job, but when she described it to me later, we realized it went beyond unusual.

Mrs. Barrett opened the door the moment Mary Anne knocked. She was beaming and without saying a word she held out her left hand. A beautiful ring sparkled on her third finger.

"Oh," gasped Mary Anne. "An engagement ring!"

Mrs. Barrett nodded and stepped back. "Yes. The night of that cocktail party. He asked me then. It was so wonderful."

Mary Anne remembered that was the night that Claudia and Stacey had been sitting for the seven kids, and she remembered how happy the two adults had been acting. So that's what it was! Love and a marriage proposal.

"Ooh, this is *so* exciting!" cried Mary Anne. She was totally thrilled. A proposal meant a wedding, and to Mary Anne, the world's most romantic and sensitive person, a wedding is a world-class event. Mary Anne threw her arms around Mrs. Barrett and gave her a big hug.

Then she began to fire a million questions at Mrs. Barrett, like when was the wedding, and where, and where would they live, and would there be bridesmaids, and what was Mrs. Barrett going to wear.

"Whoa," said Mrs. Barrett, laughing. "The wedding is in December. Let's see — we'll all be moving into one house. I'll take DeWitt for my new surname, but Buddy, Suzi, and Marnie will stay Barretts, of course. Buddy will be the ringbearer and Lindsey will be the flowergirl. I don't know what I'm wearing yet. Or what flowers I'll carry," she added, anticipating Mary Anne's next question.

Mary Anne nodded but her mind was already racing ahead. "The BSC will help any way it can," she promised (meaning that she especially would be glad to help with a wedding).

Mrs. Barrett looked pleased. "Why, thank you, Mary Anne. That's very sweet of you."

"This is so, so, so great," said Mary Anne, clasping her hands together.

"I think so, too," Mrs. Barrett said, looking suddenly shy and actually blushing a little. Then she looked at her watch, shook her wrist, held her watch to her ear and cried, "It is accurate. Oh, I am *late!*"

Mrs. Barrett practically flew out the door and it wasn't until Mary Anne had waved good-bye that she realized that in all her excitement over the upcoming wedding possibilities, she hadn't seen a single Barrett kid. She knew Marnie was taking a nap, but where were Buddy and Suzi? At least one of them usually met her at the door when she arrived.

"Buddy?" she called (not too loudly, so she wouldn't wake up Marnie). "Suzi?"

No one answered, but she heard the sound of the television from the den.

Sure enough, Buddy and Suzi were sitting on the sofa in front of the television.

"Hey," said Mary Anne, walking in. "What is this? Celebrity Mud Wrestling? I don't believe it!"

Buddy just kept staring straight ahead at the TV, his arms folded and his lower lip poked out. So did Suzi.

"You guys, are you telling me you find mud wrestling more interesting than me? That hurts!"

Suzi flashed Mary Anne a look out of the corner of her eyes. "You're glad she's getting married!" she said. "We heard you!"

Well, *that* caught Mary Anne off guard. She'd been so into the whole wedding scenario that she'd forgotten that Buddy and Suzi might not feel the same way.

"Oh. Yes, I am glad for your mother. She seems very happy," Mary Anne answered carefully.

"Well, we're not!" Buddy burst out. "I hate all those DeWitts."

"Me, too!" echoed Suzi.

"And I don't want any more brothers and sisters, either."

"Me, too." That was Suzi again.

"Wow," said Mary Anne softly, looking at the two highly agitated and *very* cross children in front of her. She pointed at the TV. "Do you mind if I turn this off?"

"Okay," said Buddy grudgingly.

Mary Anne turned off the television, then turned to face the Barretts.

"You know, my father got married again," she began. "And I got a new family when he did. Now I have a new sister who is also one of my best friends and . . ."

She didn't get to finish.

"No!" said Buddy. "NO! NO! NO!"

"I don't want to share my room with them," cried Suzi. "I like my room. It's *my* room."

"It's not so bad to share . . ." Mary Anne tried again.

"And it's our house," said Buddy. "We don't need them in our house." He bounced up off the sofa and looked around. "I know. I know what we can do."

"What?" Suzi bounced up, too.

"We can DeWitt-proof the house. Like in that old movie, *Swiss Family Robinson*, when they build all those traps for the pirates, remember?"

Mary Anne tried to look stern, but inside she was stifling a sympathetic laugh. The DeWitts as pirates? Good grief!

"Yes!" Suzi nodded emphatically. "DeWitt traps!"

With that, Buddy was off.

Rather than try to talk Buddy and Suzi out of their project, Mary Anne decided to let them work some steam out of their systems for awhile, tagging along to keep an eye on things to make sure they didn't get out of hand. And maybe she could gradually make Buddy and Suzi see reason while she was at it. Then Mrs. Barrett could talk to them when she got home and help Buddy and Suzi de-DeWitt-proof the house before the dinner party.

Buddy and Suzi's first project was DeWitt-proofing their rooms. While Mary Anne watched, the two kids filled pans with water and put them just inside the door, tied strings to the door handles, and attached them to the backs of chairs so that the chairs would tip over when the doors were opened. Then they made big signs that said, "DeWitts keep out, or else!"

"There," said Buddy, helping Suzi tape up the last corner of her sign on her door. "That should do it."

"It looks effective," said Mary Anne truthfully.

Buddy looked around, then said, "Ha!" A moment later he was carefully rubbing vaseline on the doorknob of the bathroom he and Suzi shared. "See, I'm leaving this part in the back without vaseline," he explained to Suzi. "So we can open it, 'cause we know the secret."

Suzi nodded and helped Buddy make a sign that said, "Barrett bathroom *only*."

Next came the den. Buddy and Suzi made signs and put them on the chairs and sofa: Buddy's, Suzi's, Marnie's.

"You know," Mary Anne tried again. "Kristy's family is a combined family and it's great. They have a lot of fun. There are as many as *ten* people in Kristy's house sometimes, not counting their pets. It's always interesting. Something amazing is always happening."

It was like talking to a wall. Buddy said, "I guess we can't put signs on all the chairs. We'll have to fix the other chairs special."

"I know!" cried Suzi. She charged off and returned a minute later with towels and a big container of cornstarch baby powder. Spreading the white towels across the seats of the

96

unlabelled chairs, she dusted them liberally with powder.

"When they sit down, it'll make a big puff!" she said happily.

"Excellent!" said Buddy.

The rest of the afternoon went like that. The Barretts went from room to room, labeling things, making DeWitt traps (although Mary Anne stopped them from doing things like putting buckets of water on the edges of partly opened doors) and ignoring any positive thing Mary Anne might have to say about her combined family or Kristy's, or about how much fun weddings might be.

Finally she gave up, got Marnie up from her nap, and changed her clothes (and kept the kids from labeling Marnie as Barrett property). By the time they sat down to a snack of fruit and milk just before Mrs. Barrett was due back, the house was thoroughly DeWitt-proofed, and Mary Anne was contemplating spending at least part of the time scheduled for helping Mrs. Barrett with dinner before the DeWitts came over, taking down traps and removing signs.

Wrong.

To Mary Anne's horror, it wasn't just Mrs. Barrett who came through the door. It was Mrs. Barrett and Franklin and all four DeWitt children.

"No!" gasped Mary Anne, rising to her feet. In her usual Mrs. Barrett way, she'd changed plans on the spur of the moment.

"We can *all* cook dinner together!" Mrs. Barrett announced cheerfully.

"Ha," said Buddy.

Mary Anne managed to head them off for a moment by persuading the DeWitt kids to sit down for a snack (Buddy and Suzi unceremoniously got up and went back to the den). But she wasn't able to catch Mrs. Barrett's eye and warn her, so Mary Ann flew through the house, snatching down signs and deactivating "traps."

But she wasn't fast enough. Suddenly she heard a shriek from the den. She raced in to see Lindsey sitting on one of the towel-covered chairs, a cloud of white powder floating in the air around her and powder all over her face and hair.

Buddy and Suzi burst out laughing. Then Taylor, who'd come in behind Mary Anne, saw the signs on the chairs. "What does that mean?" Taylor asked, pointing.

"That DeWitts aren't welcome in *our* house. Or *our* family. We don't need you. So there!" said Buddy.

"Buddy!" said Mary Anne.

Another cry sounded in the hall and Madeleine came in crying "Euw, euw, euwwww" and holding out her hands. Lindsey looked at Madeleine's hands and said, "Gross. She's got slimy stuff all over her hands."

"The sign said that bathroom was for Barretts only. That'll teach you to use our stuff without permission!" declared Suzi.

"Fine!" said Lindsey. "We don't want anything to do with your stupid stuff or your stupid family, anyway. You can go, go, go fry your head in peanut butter."

The DeWitts marched out, leaving Buddy and Suzi looking angry but triumphant.

Miraculously, Mrs. Barrett and Franklin didn't seem to have yet noticed anything amiss. They were in the kitchen beginning preparations for dinner. Mary Anne helped, and, every chance she got, dashed out to move another sign or take apart another booby trap. But by the time she got ready to go, she hadn't succeeded in finding them all.

She left Franklin and Mrs. Barrett in the kitchen, talking and laughing as they chopped vegetables for beef stew, while the Barretts sat in the den with the DeWitts, playing a silent, deadly game of Monopoly in the living room.

"Mine, mine, mine!" she heard Taylor say as she walked out the door.

"You know, I don't think Buddy and Suzi are too happy with the idea of sharing their family with the DeWitts," Mary Anne said to Mrs. Barrett as she left.

"That's all right, dear," said Mrs. Barrett. "They like the DeWitts."

Mary Anne sighed. She'd tried. There was nothing she could do.

But she sensed a disastrous evening ahead for the Barretts and the DeWitts.

CHAPTER 10

"Here," I said. I passed Whitney the sunblock and leaned back with a sigh. Another perfect California day, and Whitney and I were celebrating by spending the whole afternoon outdoors in the shade of a tree.

Of course, it's hard to get sunburned sitting under a tree, but I knew how easily Whitney burned and I wasn't taking any chances. Whitney reminded me a little of the time Kristy's little sister Karen had decided to become instantly grown-up by copying everything she saw Kristy and the other members of the BSC do. If Whitney saw me putting on sunblock, she put it on, too, without a question.

I pushed my sunglasses up on my nose and sighed a sigh of perfect contentment.

Whitney pushed her glasses up, then frowned. "Are you unhappy, Dawn?"

Realizing that Whitney was talking about

my sigh, I smiled and said quickly, "No way. That was a sigh of happiness."

Whitney smiled then, too. "Good," she said.

We sat silently for a little while, soaking up the soft warmth of the air and the outdoors-in-the-neighborhood noises all around us: someone washing a car (not as energy efficient as a car wash, but just this once I'd overlook it), birds, the distant sound of a dog barking, the rhythmic *snap-snap-snap* of hand shears from someone trimming a hedge (the old-fashioned way, without electricity).

Then Whitney said, "I'm hungry."

"Mmm," I said. "Not now, Whitney."

"I want another ice-cream sandwich."

"You had one right after your mother left this afternoon. Why don't you wait until your parents get home and have another one after dinner?" I asked. What I didn't want to say was that Whitney simply couldn't have another ice-cream sandwich. The last thing Mrs. Cater had said to me before she left earlier was, "We're going out to dinner this evening, so don't let Whitney eat anything after three o'clock. I don't want her to spoil her appetite."

In a normal baby-sitting situation, I could have said, "I'm sorry, you can't have another ice-cream sandwich, Whitney. Your parents said so, and I'm responsible for seeing to it

102

that you do what they say. That's the rule."

"I don't want to wait until after dinner," Whitney answered. Then she added coaxingly, "Aren't you hungry, too, Dawn?"

I laughed and shook my head. "I don't have your sweet tooth, Whitney."

That distracted Whitney for a minute. "What's a sweet tooth?"

"Oh. It's, well, it's just a way of saying that you like to eat sweet things a lot."

"I do," agreed Whitney, nodding again. She reached up and tapped her finger against one of her front teeth and laughed loudly.

Then she jumped to her feet and headed for the back door.

"Whitney? Whitney!" I called. I jumped to my feet and headed after her.

She was opening the freezer door when I caught up with her.

"Whitney, no. You can't have another ice cream sandwich." I put my hand on the freezer door and closed it firmly.

Just as firmly, Whitney kept her fingers wrapped around the door handle. "I *want* another ice-cream sandwich," she said stubbornly.

"Just wait a little while, okay?" I said.

Whitney sighed.

Taking that as acceptance of my words, I took my hand off the door.

Quickly Whitney yanked the door open and grabbed the box of ice-cream sandwiches.

Even more quickly, I grabbed the box from Whitney's hands. "No!" I said, more sharply than I had intended. I shoved the box back in the freezer, closed the door, and turned to face an infuriated Whitney.

"I can too have another sandwich. I can have as many as I want. You're not the boss of me!" cried Whitney.

"Whitney, I am your baby-sitter and I — " I stopped in horror, clapping my hand over my mouth.

But it was too late.

Whitney's eyes widened. Her expression grew stricken. "You're my *baby-sitter*?" she repeated incredulously.

"Uh, well, it's not exactly that," I began lamely. What could I say? I could lie, try to pretend it was a big joke.

But I knew that Whitney would know. She'd know I was lying and that would hurt her feelings even more.

"Dawn?" asked Whitney.

"I — " I looked into Whitney's eyes. I knew she knew.

"Yes, I'm your baby-sitter. Your parents hired me to stay with you in the afternoons until your camp starts. They didn't want you to be alone."

The stricken look left Whitney's face, to be replaced by one of humiliation. And anger. And betrayal.

"Oh, Whitney. It's not what you think. I mean, I . . ."

"I thought you were my friend!" Whitney yelled."I thought you were my *friend!*"

The last word ended on a long, drawn out wail as Whitney turned and stomped out of the room.

"Whitney, wait! I *am* your friend. Whitney?"

The sound of a door slamming and being locked was my only answer.

"Whitney spent the rest of the afternoon in her room and nothing I said or did could get her to come out or even to answer me.

After her mother returned, I talked to Mrs. Cater for a little while. She wasn't too upset. She just shook her head and said, "Maybe it wasn't the best way to go about it after all. But it's not your fault, Dawn. Just give her time." I went to say good-bye to Whitney through the door. It opened then, and for a moment I hoped Whitney had forgiven me.

I was wrong. Her face wooden, her eyes accusing, Whitney said, "Give me back the necklace."

"The Best Friends necklace? Whitney, you don't mean that, do you?"

Wrong question.

"I do!" Whitney yelled, her eyes filling with tears. "I mean it forever."

And when I'd given her back the necklace, she slammed the door again and locked me out once more.

I thought of Whitney all that night. I felt terrible: terrible about the lie, terrible about how badly I had handled the whole thing.

I tried to imagine how Whitney must feel. As an imaginary feeling, it was pretty awful. For Whitney it must have been a hundred times worse.

The next morning, I called Mrs. Cater as early as I could.

"How is Whitney?" I asked.

"She stayed in her room all night," Mrs. Cater told me. Her voice sounded sad and tired. "I'm so sorry that this happened."

"If only I'd been more careful," I said.

"No. No, we should have told Whitney right from the start. But she works so hard at being 'grown-up' and self-reliant and we wanted to give her support in that. We were afraid saying you were her baby-sitter would undermine that positive self-image." Mrs. Cater paused, then went on in a tone of forced cheerfulness, "Still, Whitney is always so sweet and good-natured. She'll get over it. I'm sure of that."

"Should I come this afternoon?"

"Yes. Yes, you need to be here. And maybe that will help," Mrs. Cater told me.

So as usual, I went to the Caters' that afternoon.

"Whitney's in her room," said Mrs. Cater, who met me at the door.

"Is she . . ."

Mrs. Cater nodded. "But the door is open. That's a good sign, I think."

I certainly hoped so. As soon as Mrs. Cater had gone, I went to Whitney's room.

Whitney was sitting on the floor, looking at a magazine.

"Hi, Whitney!" I said.

No answer.

"Is that a good magazine? I don't think I've seen that one yet."

I might as well have been talking to myself.

Although I kept trying, Whitney didn't speak to me the entire afternoon.

Or the next.

Then on the third afternoon, she looked up from the puzzle she was doing and said, "I'm not a baby. I don't need a baby-sitter."

Taking this as an opening, I said, "You're not a baby. That's true. Baby-sitter isn't the word I should have used."

Whitney turned her back to me.

She didn't speak to me again until I saw her go by with a basketful of laundry.

"What's happening?" I said.

Whitney kept going, headed for the laundry room. I followed her. I watched as she sorted out the clothes and began to put them into the washing machine.

"Want some help?" I asked.

"I'm not a baby," said Whitney. "I can do it myself."

After that, no matter what happened, Whitney seemed determined to prove that she didn't need any help at all with anything, determined to prove that she was grown-up and didn't need me at all.

After a dozen attempts to join Whitney in whatever she was doing or to coax her into joining me, and being told, "I'm not a baby. I don't need a baby-sitter," I gave up.

At least on that approach.

I had hurt Whitney and there was nothing I could do to change that. All I could do now was wait and hope she could work things out for herself.

And then maybe she would forgive me.

CHAPTER 11

"Take me out to the old ball game," my father sang, loudly and off-key.

I winced.

Jeff said, "Daaaad."

Dad stopped singing and pulled his jacket on. "Kayla's job with the public relations firm is not only challenging, but it has special perks. The tickets she got for us this evening are prime seats."

Those words brought out the more tolerant side of Jeff. "Cool," he said.

I didn't say anything. I like baseball, don't get me wrong. But I wasn't sure I liked the idea of spending a whole evening at a California Angels game all the way over in Anaheim.

"What's Kayla like?" I asked as I followed Dad and Jeff to the car.

"She's in public relations," my father told me. Again.

"And she likes baseball?" I said.

"Looks that way," my father agreed. He concentrated on backing out of the driveway, then said casually, over his shoulder, "By the way, Kayla's daughter will be joining us. Kayla loved the idea of a family date and wanted Alana to come, too."

Alana. That was an unusual name. I'd only met one other person with that name, a classmate who was sort of a pain. No, wrong, who was a *big* pain.

But it probably wasn't the same Alana, I told myself. Couldn't be. It was one thing to believe in ghosts, another to believe in wild coincidences.

Maybe Alana wasn't such an unusual name after all. Maybe it was one of those popular names for an upcoming generation, the way Jennifer had been. Maybe I just hadn't heard about the new name-your-kid-Alana trend. I fervently hoped so.

Wrong. Alana was *the* Alana. Alana the Pain-a from my school.

I could tell she was just as thrilled to see me.

Kayla slid into the car next to our father and turned to smile at us. She had a nice smile. She and Alana sort of looked alike, too.

But if Alana had a smile like her mother's,

we weren't going to find out about it that night.

Alana opened the car door, looked in, and said in a completely flat voice, "It *is* you."

Any thought I'd had of welcoming her died right there. I folded my arms and turned to stare out the window.

It was so totally weird. It wasn't as if Alana and I were total enemies. We weren't. We didn't even know each other that well.

But we hung out in completely different crowds. Alana's crowd could have been labeled "Brain Trust," or "Rocket Scientists of the Future." She and her friends made straight A's, were always winning merit awards and honorable mentions and doing extra work for extra credit. They sat together at the same table in the caf and talked more quietly and seriously than everybody else. But if you listened to their conversations, they didn't sound like conversations at all. The words were big and the concepts were complicated, but it seemed more as if they were showing off how much they knew than enjoying knowing it.

Not like me and my friends: study hard, work hard (and be great baby-sitters), play hard, and don't forget to surf. That could have been our motto. Needless to say, we made more noise at our lunch table.

And I didn't have to be a future rocket scientist to know that Alana and her crowd looked down on us for being the way we were.

I wasn't happy with this set-up. I didn't think Alana was, either.

But I did try, at least a little. After a few minutes, I cleared my throat and said, in Alana's general direction, "So, do you like baseball?"

"It's a silly game," said Alana.

I frowned. She was calling my father and Jeff — and her mother — silly. And me, too, for that matter, even if I wasn't as big a baseball fan as my brother and father.

Still, I decided to try to be polite. "I can see how people might not like baseball," I said. "What sports do you like?"

Alana looked over at me and raised one eyebrow. Her expression was disdainful. "Sports don't interest me," she said.

"Oh," I said.

I could take a hint.

I leaned forward and said to Kayla, "Do you like sports?"

Kayla smiled at me and nodded. "You're not going to believe this, but I used to be on my fencing team in college."

"There's a sport for you, Dawn," said Alana sarcastically.

Her mother ignored her and went on,

"These days, I make do with tennis."

"Fencing?" I said, impressed. "Was it hard?"

"Wow. What an incisive question," muttered Alana.

I bared my teeth in what wasn't a smile and turned to Alana. "What did you say, Alana?"

Everyone was quiet. Then Alana said. "Nothing." She turned to look out the window.

Dad cleared his throat. "Here we are," he said.

At the stadium, Dad and Kayla had plenty to say about where to park the car. I could see, a little, where Alana got her manner of speaking. Kayla had the same sort of sarcastic way of saying things. It bothered me, but I figured that my Dad knew where she was coming from and could handle it. For that matter, I knew where Alana was coming from — the Brain Trust snobs — and I could handle that. I just hated to waste a whole evening on it.

At last Dad and Kayla compromised on a parking spot, and we were on our way into the game.

If you've ever been to a baseball game, you know that the roar of the crowd and the smell of hot dogs are two big, big factors. The roar of the crowd I can take, but not the hot dogs.

So when Dad rounded up dogs with mustard and kraut for Alana, Kayla, Jeff, and himself (although I knew he and Jeff weren't big dog fans), I was prepared. I opened my backpack and brought out an avocado spread and sprout sandwich, a whole wheat blueberry muffin, and an orange.

"What *is* that green stuff?" Alana's voice cut into my satisfied contemplation of my healthy baseball game food.

"Avocado spread," I said. "Do you want to try some?"

"You've *got* to be kidding," said Alana. "I can't believe anyone would be so weird as to bring health food to a baseball game."

Then she took a big bite of hot dog.

I couldn't help it. I made a disgusting gagging sound.

Alana got a pained look on her face and swallowed quickly. Then she turned her back on me.

"You girls doing all right?" my father asked.

"Sure, Jack," said Alana.

Jack? Since when did Alana call my father Jack?

But Dad didn't seen to notice. He nodded and turned his attention back to the stadium. A moment later, he was leaping to his feet, trying to get a wave started, cheering loudly.

Under her breath, Alana muttered, "Jerk."

"What did you say?" I heard my voice go up.

Alana gave me a small superior smile. "Shh. You don't want to upset Jack the jerk, do you?"

I couldn't believe my ears. "What?" I repeated, leaning forward.

Alana opened her mouth. And shrieked as I dumped my lemon-lime seltzer in her lap.

"You did that on purpose!" she sputtered, scrubbing at the wet spot with her napkin.

"Alana the genius," I retorted, giving her a mean smile.

The game went on forever. Alana and I warily ignored one another for nine long innings. Dad spent the time shouting things like "Good play!" and having Kayla say things like, "You call that a good play, Jack? Really? How — interesting."

After we dropped Alana and Kayla off, no one needed to say it aloud: the family date had been a big strike out.

Jeff and I settled in for the Saturday midnight monster movie. Dad, looking discouraged, said, "I'm going to call it a night. See you guys tomorrow."

After he'd left, Jeff said, "Yuk."

"Double yuk," I said. "Where does Dad find these people?"

"The supermarket," Jeff answered. "The video store. Work."

"Yeah, and Monsters are Us," I added. I paused then went on, "Remember Carol?"

"Yeah," said Jeff.

We were both silent for a moment, thinking about Carol. She and Dad had actually been engaged. But then they'd decided they weren't compatible and called it off.

Jeff and I hadn't been all that crazy about Dad remarrying and we hadn't given Carol much of a chance. I wondered now if maybe we hadn't been wrong. All Carol had ever done was try too hard to be nice — something any normal person might do, especially if she loved someone and wanted his family to like her.

Normal. All these people we'd had family dates with had been "normal." Nice, normal people who were nasty to people who were different from them, or full of weird rules and regulations, or just plain obnoxious.

I was sick of normal people. Dad deserved someone better than that. Someone like Carol.

I looked at Jeff. He looked at me. I knew we were thinking the same thing.

"We've got to get Carol and Dad back together," I said aloud.

Jeff put up his hand, and we gave each other the high-five.

CHAPTER 12

Saturday

Well, we've been house hunting.

Yes, It's important to have a big house, when you have a big family.

You're the expert, Kristy! After all, you not only have a big family, you have a ghost relative who has his own room!

True, Shannon. Good thing I didn't mention that to the Barrett and the DeWitt kids, though. They might have used that as one of their requirements for picking out a new house: resident ghost required.

It's not too much to ask, is it? After all, when Dawn and Mary Anne's family got together, they got to live in a haunted house.

Also true. Wait'll we write to Dawn about all this...

In spite of the war between the Barretts and the DeWitts, the wedding between Mrs. Barrett and Mr. DeWitt was still on. Kristy had been hearing some of the details of the wedding, since her mom and Mrs. Barrett were friends. Of course Kristy, being Kristy, hadn't paid much attention to important details like who was wearing what and what the flowers were going to be. But she did remember to tell the BSC that the Barretts and the DeWitts were *not* going to live together in one or the other of the two families' houses. Instead, they were going to buy a new, bigger house for the whole family. They'd never planned that one of the families would share the other's house, because they knew that it would be a tight squeeze and it would also mean that whichever family moved into the other's house would thereafter be viewed as interlopers.

Mary Anne was particularly relieved to hear the news, since she'd seen the DeWitt proofing incident first-hand.

As it turned out, not only were Mrs. Barrett and Mr. DeWitt buying a new house, they were also going to include the seven kids in the house-hunting. And they called the BSC for assistance on the first house-hunting outing.

Shannon and Kristy got the job.

118

When they got to the Barretts' that Saturday morning, Franklin and his four kids had already arrived in an enormous blue van.

"Cool wheels," Kristy said to Lindsey, who was sitting in one of the seats by an open window.

Lindsey made a face. Taylor and Madeleine had gotten out and were playing a half-hearted game of tag in the front yard. Ryan was asleep in his car seat.

Mrs. Barrett, holding Marnie, was just coming out the front door with Suzi and Buddy.

Shannon leaped forward and she and Kristy began to help get seven kids (and two adults) organized for the house-hunting trip.

It was not an easy thing. Suzi opened the van door and hopped in, claiming the window seat behind the driver. Taylor immediately said, "That's my seat."

"Ha," said Buddy, rushing to his sister's defense. "Is your name written on it?"

"No, but it's our father's van, so we get first choice."

"Mom, is that true?" wailed Suzi. "I get car sick if I can't look out the window."

"It's true," said Mrs. Barrett, starting to look frazzled all ready.

"Oooh! Car sick. I'm not sitting next to Suzi," said Taylor, abruptly reversing his position. "She stinks."

"I do not!" shouted Suzi.

"Well, I'm not sitting next to *any* DeWitts. You *all* stink," said Buddy.

"Not like the Barrett Stink Bombs," Lindsey said.

"Enough!" said Kristy, in her best no-nonsense voice.

It silenced both the Barretts and the De-Witts. Soon she and Shannon had all seven kids seated (with Kristy and Shannon in between so that no Barrett was sitting next to a DeWitt and vice versa.)

Shannon said, as they pulled out of the driveway, "It's sort of like one of those math problems in school, you know?"

"Yeah," said Kristy, giving Buddy, who was leaning forward to stick his tongue out at Taylor, a warning look. Buddy leaned back. "Don't ask me how we did it, though!"

She and Shannon thought they were going to have to spend the rest of the house-hunting expedition acting as referees. But midway into the tour of the first house, they realized they were wrong.

The real estate agent kept his smile firmly in place as the van pulled up to the first house, a split level ranch house with a fenced-in back-yard, and seven kids, two baby-sitters, and two adults spilled out. "Ah," he said. "How delightful. What a lovely family you have here."

Shannon and Kristy looked at the agent as if he were nuts, since the DeWitts and the Barretts had taken advantage of the new territory to draw up new lines of battle ("I'm not walking next to her!" "Oh, he has cooties. He touched me, he touched me!")

"I'm sure we have the perfect house for you," the agent went on, leading the way down the wide, straight front walk.

Buddy paused to look up and down the sidewalk. "It's a good sidewalk for skateboards," he noted. "Smooth. Good curb."

Lindsey stopped, too, as if struck by what Buddy had said. She studied the sidewalk for a moment from a couple of angles and then said, "You're right."

It soon became clear that the kids and the adults were looking for somewhat different things in a house.

"Notice the number of closets," the agent said, throwing open a closet door as if he'd built it himself especially for Mr. DeWitt and Mrs. Barrett.

"Wow, look at that! A tree house!" cried Suzi, running to press her face against the sliding glass door that led from the kitchen onto the back deck.

"Neat," cried Taylor, coming to stand beside her. "Look, Madeleine," he said to his sister, whose hand he was holding. "A tree house."

"May we go look?" Buddy asked Mrs. Barrett.

"Of course, of course," said the agent, his big fake smile growing bigger. "It's very sturdy. Has a safety rail around it."

"A lovely view from the kitchen," said Mr. DeWitt as the four kids raced out, followed by Kristy holding Ryan, and Shannon holding Marnie.

"Look at this!" exclaimed Buddy a moment later, leaning on the rail. "You can see *everything*."

While the adults toured the rest of the house, the kids compared notes on the tree house and the backyard.

"Look, it even has a dog house!" cried Lindsey.

"But we don't have a dog now," said Suzi, looking distressed.

"It can be a guest dog house," said Lindsey. "Like a dog hotel."

"And we could use the dog house as a fort-in-disguise," said Buddy.

"Time to go," said Mr. DeWitt.

Everyone piled back in the van, but with a lot fewer complaints and disputes.

"No tree house," said Buddy immediately at the next house.

"Five lovely bedrooms," said the agent, smiling and smiling. "And three baths, including a bath in the master bedroom."

"There are seven of us," said Suzi. "Who gets their own bedroom?"

"Marnie and Ryan can share. They're little. They won't mind," said Buddy.

"Ohh, look at this little room," said Suzi. "It's cute."

"I like this big one," said Taylor. "It has cool window seats."

"Me, too," said Buddy. He and Taylor looked at each other and so did Shannon and Kristy, waiting for the fight to break out.

Then Buddy said, "We could put a terrarium in one of the windows."

Taylor nodded. "Neat," he said.

After that, the kids raced up to each house as if it were a big adventure. While the adults talked about things like dry basements and insulation and solar heating and access to schools, Buddy and Suzi and Taylor and Lindsey and sometimes Madeleine and Marnie and Ryan looked at backyards from a kid's point of view; rated trees for climbing and treehouse potential; timed how long it took to run around the house for future race potential; checked out sidewalks for skateboard, Rollerblade, and bicycle possibilities; and peppered the real estate agent with questions about whether they could slide down bannisters and how many containers of ice cream would fit in the freezer in the refrigerator. They were particularly impressed by one house that had a whole separate freezer in the basement. By Buddy's estimate, it would hold enough ice cream for an entire year.

By the time the house-hunting expedition was over, the only point of serious disagreement was over what kind of ice cream to put in the freezer.

"Maybe we'll get a farm," cried Suzi, her eyes shining. "With horses and goats."

"Horses, horses," said Marnie, catching her sister's enthusiasm.

"Or a house with a swimming pool," suggested Lindsey.

"Or a farm with a pond," said Buddy.

"For swimming or fishing," Taylor added.

Listening to them talk, Shannon and Kristy were relieved to see that the war between the Barretts and DeWitts was over. From her own experience, Kristy knew that the road ahead would not always be smooth. But the first part, in some ways the hardest part, accepting that things were going to change and looking for the good possibilities in the changes, had begun.

They were on their way to making a new family.

CHAPTER 13

Clover was holding a bowl on her head — right side up. Daffodil was running after her with the hose, trying to fill the bowl up. Both girls were wearing their bathing suits and the sprinkler was on full force.

"I'm wet, I'm wet," shrieked Clover, and I smiled.

I was baby-sitting for the Austins and I couldn't think of a better place to be on such a hot, hot day.

Still, watching them race through the sprinklers made me tired and thirsty. I decided it was about time they took a break.

"Clover! Daf! Water-break!" I called.

Clover went into peals of laughter and so did Daffodil. "That's funny, Dawn!" shouted Clover.

"No, really, I mean it. Let's take a rest and drink some juice."

"Five more minutes," pleaded Daffodil.

The two stopped and turned to look at me pleadingly.

"I'll get the juice and come back out," I said. "Stay in the backyard, okay?"

"Okay," said Clover instantly. She took advantage of the moment to dash the contents of her bowl of water on her older sister. Instantly, the two took off through the sprinklers again.

Smiling and shaking my head, I went inside to fix some orange juice.

Five minutes later I came out onto the back steps. "Juic . . ." I called. My voice trailed off.

The sprinklers were off. And Clover and Daffodil were nowhere in sight.

I put the tray of juice and glasses down on the table by the steps and checked the backyard quickly. Both girls' sneakers and T-shirts were gone from the lawn chair where they had tossed them.

"Clover! Daffodil!" I called.

No answer. Nevertheless, I checked around the front and the backyard in case they were hiding, playing a game. But although I looked in every possible place and listened carefully for stifled giggles, I found (and heard) no sign of the two girls.

I didn't panic. Friends had probably come by and the girls, forgetting their promise to stay in the yard, had gone to play with them.

But although there were a number of kids up the street, no one had seen Daffodil or Clover.

My heart was beginning to pound heavily now. I had to force myself to stay calm as I returned to the Austins' house and checked it carefully one more time.

No Daffodil. No Clover.

I raced back out of the house and down the sidewalk, headed for a group of kids at the other end of the block. They were older boys, unlikely to play with Daf or Clover, but I thought they might have seen something. I was running so fast that I almost knocked over a little boy standing and watching the big boys play basketball.

"Whoa! Sorry," I gasped, grabbing him before he toppled backward. "Are you okay?"

He gave me a scornful look, refusing to act like a little kid in front of the big kids. " 'Course I am."

On impulse, I said, "You haven't seen two girls go this way? One about your age?" I described what Daffodil and Clover were wearing.

To my surprise — and relief — the little boy nodded.

"Where?" I asked.

He pointed up the sidewalk. "They were walking with a lady," he said.

"What lady?" I asked. My heart started to hammer. "What did she look like? Tall? Short? Brown hair? Gray hair?"

But he shook his head stubbornly. "A lady. That's all. Just a lady."

Had Daffodil and Clover been kidnapped? I couldn't believe they'd go somewhere with a complete stranger. But I didn't know what else to think, and I couldn't take any chances. And Mrs. Austin couldn't be reached right away. She was at an outdoors crafts fair exhibiting her weaving and wouldn't be back until early evening.

I called the police.

They were there in no time. And before long, a whole group of neighbors, plus my father and Jeff, had spread out to search for Clover and Daffodil.

"I can't believe it," I kept saying. "They were in the backyard. Inside the fence. I just went indoors for a second."

My father patted my shoulder. "Don't worry, Sunshine. They'll turn up. There's probably a perfectly logical explanation for all this."

I wanted to believe him. But I couldn't.

I raced up and down the streets, calling their names. Then, realizing that I was just covering the same ground that the neighborhood search party was covering, I left the neighborhood, still calling, still looking.

But with less and less hope.

Eventually, I found myself looking up at a Ferris wheel. It was the last day of the carnival, the one we'd gone to on that disastrous family date with Clarice when I'd gotten the lime green toy I'd given to Whitney.

Like the whirling in my brain, the Ferris wheel circled and circled. What was I going to do? How was I going to tell Mrs. Austin?

Suddenly, my eyes focused. And I couldn't believe what I was seeing. Because going around and around on the Ferris wheel were Daffodil and Clover Austin. Whitney Cater was sitting in the middle with one of the girls on either side.

I was so astonished, I didn't know what to do.

Clover saw me and shouted, "DAWWW-WN!" She waved wildly, beaming.

Daffodil smiled, too. Whitney looked at me without any expression at all.

When the Ferris wheel touched down and the girls got off, I rushed up to them. "There you are!" I cried.

"It's so much fun!" cried Clover. "We're going to the funhouse next."

Realizing that they didn't even know they

were missing, I took a deep breath. "Maybe in a little while. But right now, we need to get back home. Come on."

"Clover and Daffodil are good," said Whitney, hanging back a little.

"Come on, Whitney," I said. "Help me walk them home."

Whitney nodded and fell into step beside us. I spotted a police officer ahead. "Wait here," I said.

I raced up to the officer and, never taking my eyes off the three as they stood at a little distance, told her what had happened. The officer nodded. "That's what usually happens," she said, getting out her radio to call off the search. "I'm glad that was the case this time, too."

Clover, who had pulled the other two closer, yanked on my arm. "We weren't lost!" she said indignantly. "We were with Whitney!"

"I took care of them," Whitney said. "I was baby-sitting."

"See?" said Clover.

"What happened?" I asked.

"Whitney came by and asked us to go to the carnival while you were inside. She said she was baby-sitting. We thought it would be okay," said Daffodil.

"But first I made them turn off the sprinklers

and put on their shirts and sneakers," said Whitney. "That was right."

"Yes, that *was* right," I said. "But you shouldn't have gone anywhere without telling me."

Just then, I looked up and saw a familiar face. "Carol?" I said.

"Dawn! I thought that was you. My girl-friend and I were just buying some cotton candy and I saw you over here. Are you having fun?"

"Ah . . . well," I said.

Carol turned to Whitney and held out her hand. "Hi, I'm Carol."

"How do you do," said Whitney. "I'm Whitney. This is Clover and Daffodil."

"Yes, I'm glad to see you all," said Carol, smiling at them. "You know, Whitney, I watched you earlier on the merry-go-round. You looked like you were having fun."

Carol turned back to me and said, "She was very responsible, making sure the girls didn't get on animals that were too big for them. And she wouldn't let them go on the Zipper."

"See?" said Whitney. "See? I *am* grown-up! I'm grown-up enough to baby-sit."

By now, I knew what had happened. Whitney had wanted to prove that she could baby-sit, too, that she was grown-up. And she *had* done a good job, except that she had taken Clover and Daffodil without telling anyone.

"We've got to go," I said aloud. "It's good to see you again, Carol."

"It's good to see you," Carol told me, and to my surprise, she leaned over and gave me a quick, impulsive hug.

That night, after all the excitement was over, I remembered to tell Dad I'd seen Carol at the carnival.

"It was great to see her," I said. "She was terrific. And she was really nice to Whitney."

My father looked pleased. "I'm glad," he said.

"You know," I said slowly. "Maybe you should call her."

I looked down at the toe of my shoe, then up at my father. He wasn't looking at me. He was staring into space, rubbing his chin, a thoughtful smile on his face.

CHAPTER 14

It was time for Whitney and me to have a talk, I decided as I walked over to the Caters' house to begin my last week of baby-sitting for Whitney. The following Monday, Whitney's day camp program was going to begin. If Whitney and I didn't settle what had happened between us, we might never get it sorted out at all.

As soon as Mr. Cater left for work, I walked over to where Whitney was sitting by the window in the den. She hadn't said hello when I'd come in, but at least she didn't have her back turned to me.

"Whitney, we have to talk," I said.

Whitney looked at me, but she didn't say anything.

"Okay. Okay, listen. You took really good care of Clover and Daffodil. You were very responsible with them. Everyone says so."

I took a deep breath and Whitney burst out,

"See? I can do it! I really can be grown-up! But no one ever listens to me. Especially Mom and Dad."

I didn't smile. I felt a huge twinge of sympathy. We'd all gone through that. We're still going through it, whether it was Stacey's overprotective parents not trusting her enough to be responsible about her diabetes, or Mary Anne's father keeping her in pigtails until she was practically grown-up.

Thinking hard, I told Whitney about Mary Anne and about Stacey. And about some of the things that I'd been through, too.

"All of us have had to convince our parents that we are ready for more responsibility. You have to convince your parents, too, Whitney," I concluded.

"I can! I can do things. But they won't let me!"

"You'll have to prove it to them. And I know you can. It might take time, but I know you can."

"How?" asked Whitney.

I paused. We'd all been able to make changes. And although Whitney couldn't make radical changes, some of the things that had worked for us should work for her, too.

"What about this?" I began. "Why don't you make a list of the things you know you can do now, the grown-up things. Not things you can't do, like drive a car, but real things."

Whitney nodded, watching me intently. I went on. "Then show the list to your parents and you decide together which things you can be responsible for now. You can try those things out, and if you do them, then maybe you can add more things to your grown-up list."

"My grown-up list," repeated Whitney. She nodded again and then, for the first time in days, smiled at me. "That's what I'll do, Dawn. Thank you!"

We spent the rest of the afternoon drafting the list. Holding the list in one hand, Whitney walked me to the front door as I was leaving.

I stopped and cleared my throat. "So, Whitney. Good luck with that list."

"Thank you, Dawn," said Whitney.

"There's something else. Do you think we could be friends now, as well as, well, baby-sitter and baby-sittee?"

Whitney frowned, then smiled again. "We can be both," she agreed.

"I'm glad," I said.

"Me, too," said Whitney. "Me, too."

A couple of days later, the We ♥ Kids Club met and I made a proposal: that Whitney be made an honorary club member and maybe special helper, to accompany us on some jobs, like baby-sitting for Clover and Daffodil Austin. I didn't have to convince Sunny that Whitney was great with kids.

"You should see her," she told the club. "She's super. She really plays with the kids and she's great at thinking up games. Plus she's very, very careful. Clover and Daffodil *loved* her."

Not that we needed much convincing. But Sunny's words made me feel good inside. I coughed to get everyone's attention, then called for a vote.

Unanimous. It was official. Whitney Cater was now an Honorary Member and Special Helper in the We ♥ Kids Club.

I could hardly wait to let Whitney know. I decided to tell her on the last day I sat for her.

"Let's go sit on the swings in the backyard," I suggested.

"Okay," said Whitney.

We swung back and forth for a little while. But I could tell Whitney's heart wasn't in it. After a minute or two, she stopped.

"I'm going to miss you, Dawn."

"I'll miss you, too, Whitney. But I have some good news. So maybe you won't miss me too much."

"I will miss you," insisted Whitney.

"Not if you are an Honorary Member and Special Helper in the We Love Kids Club," I

136

said. "Which you officially are. We voted you in on Wednesday. That means you'll be helping us out on special baby-sitting jobs."

Whitney's mouth opened and then closed. "A member?" she managed to say at last. "Of your club? I'm a baby-sitter!"

"Yes!"

With a whoop, Whitney pumped her swing high in the air, then jumped off, her eyes sparkling.

"Me?" she kept saying. "Me? In your club?"

"That's the deal," I said. "What do you think?"

"Yes!" shouted Whitney. Then she made herself serious for a moment. "Yes, thank you, Dawn. I'd like that."

But the seriousness couldn't last and a moment later she was dancing around me, laughing with delight.

It was a great afternoon. I didn't want it to end. But I knew now there would be other, different afternoons to which I could look forward with Whitney.

And as I was leaving, after giving Whitney a big bear hug and getting one back, I knew that Whitney and I would remain friends.

I reached up and touched the friendship necklace. Whitney had given it back to me. Friends again.

Friends forever.

CHAPTER 15

With the end of my job with Whitney, life got a little less hectic. I kicked back and invested some serious time on the beach, working on my surfing and giving my full support to the perfect days that kept arriving one after the other.

Whitney was doing well in her new day camp. And one Saturday, she and Sunny and Clover and Daffodil and I went on a special Baby-sitters excursion to the park. Needless to say, it was a big success — as good as the best surfboard ride.

Another part of life slowed down some, too. Dad stopped dating so much. He showed up for dinner more often, and even cooked a few weird Dad meals, like tofu-turkey dog casserole.

Surprise. Some things aren't meant to be eaten, even if they are good for you. We ended up going out for pizza and having a great time.

138

I wondered if that last date with Alana-the-Pain-a and Kayla had put Dad off dating forever. I wasn't sure how I felt about that. I liked having him around. But from time to time, I thought I saw a sort of lonely look on his face.

Then things picked up a bit and I knew he'd started dating again. He didn't mention her name, but Jeff and I braced ourselves for another family outing.

"Maybe it'll be to the zoo," said Jeff one night, "and we can feed her to the bears."

"Poor bears," I said, thinking back over some of the family date disasters.

We didn't ask Dad what was happening. We decided, by mutual unspoken agreement, that it was better not to know.

Then one day, Dad said casually, as he was putting on his jacket, "So, I'll be going out with someone you know tonight, guys."

Jeff clutched his throat and fell over backward. "Kayla!"

Dad smiled and shook his head.

"*Not* Karina!" I gasped.

Rolling his eyes, Dad shook his head again. "I'll put you all out of your misery. It's Carol."

"Carol! Wow," said Jeff.

"Decent," I said. I suddenly suspected that it had been Carol he'd been seeing all along now.

But Dad didn't say anything more about her after his date and he didn't mention any family dates.

Finally, one night after dinner was over, Dad began to gather up the plates. "I'll just get this into the kitchen and then we'll have dessert," he said.

"Jeff and I can get that," I said.

"Thanks," said Jeff.

"No, no," Dad insisted. "I'll get it."

He rushed back and forth, clearing the table and bringing out all the dessert stuff. Except the ice cream. Instead he sat down at the table and stared at us.

"Dad?" I prompted.

"Where's the ice cream?" asked Jeff.

"How would you feel about having Carol as your stepmother?" Dad burst out. "I know we went through this before, and I . . ."

"Carol?" said Jeff. "Carol's okay." He frowned. "Can I go get the ice cream?"

"Go get the ice cream, Jeff," I said. Good grief! Dad dishes out some major news and all Jeff can think about is ice cream.

As Jeff disappeared in the direction of the kitchen I looked at my dad. He was smiling. He looked relaxed and happy and pleased with himself.

And suddenly I was happy and pleased,

too. "I think it would be great, Dad. You and Carol."

Maybe that's what all those weird dates had been about, after all. Maybe Dad had been thinking about Carol and that's why he'd gone out with such strange people — people who couldn't possibly replace Carol.

I remembered Carol shaking hands with Whitney and smiled even more. "Great," I said again.

Jeff reappeared with ice cream and a bigger spoon for himself and we concentrated on dessert after that — on dessert and a special dinner Dad wanted to have for Carol to celebrate and "make everything official."

We spent one day planning the menu and two days getting the dinner ready, including old-fashioned Parker house rolls that had to rise *three* times, a special pasta sauce that had to sit for twenty-four hours, and three kinds of appetizers.

Carol's eyes widened when she saw the table (which we'd set up outside) with the candles and tablecloth and fresh flowers on it. "It's lovely," she said.

"For our special guest," I said, bowing a little.

Jeff snorted, but you could tell he was excited, too.

The meal went perfectly. Jeff and I kept exchanging pleased glances, but Dad just kept looking at Carol. She kept looking at him, too, and maybe she didn't taste anything we cooked after all, but she did remember to say, from time to time, "This is wonderful," and "I love this. It's delicious."

When the meal was over and we'd brought out dessert and coffee (and more milk for Jeff and raspberry seltzer for me), Dad cleared his throat.

"As you know, this is a very special occasion. We have a special guest here. She's been here before, so I don't need to introduce her."

"Is it Carol?" my brother the wit asked.

"Give the boy in the striped shirt the prize," I said. "Be quiet, Jeff."

Grinning, Jeff rolled his eyes at me. Carol saw him and smiled.

Dad went on. "But we don't want to think of Carol as a special guest anymore."

Dad stopped and suddenly sounded a lot less formal. And a lot more nervous.

"So," he said.

"Go on, Dad. You can do it," urged Jeff.

"Jeff!" I said.

"Just say it!" Jeff jumped out of his chair, threw himself on one knee, and spread his arms out. "Carol, will you marry me?" he said, and clasped his hands over his heart and fell backward.

Carol laughed and leaned forward to help Jeff up. Then she stopped and gasped. She turned to my Dad and her face grew bright pink.

"Is Jeff . . ." She began and stopped. She tried again. "Did you . . ." She stopped once more.

"Dad!" I said.

Dad's face was as pink as Carol's. "If you say yes," he said, "you'll be saying yes to me. And to these two here, too. I . . . wanted us to be in this together."

"Ohhhh!" Carol threw her arms around our father and hugged him so hard he almost fell over to join Jeff.

"It's about time," Jeff complained.

After that (while Jeff concentrated as usual on dessert), we made wedding plans. By the time Dad got up to walk Carol to her car and say good night, we knew the wedding was going to be in December, that I was going to be the maid of honor, and that Jeff was going to be the best man.

I could hardly wait.

I went to bed that night on a cloud of excitement. But I didn't go to sleep right away. I had one more thing to do to make it a perfect end to a perfect day.

I picked up the phone and punched in the number.

"Hello?" I said. "Mary Anne? It's me. Guess what? You're going to love this. There's going to be another wedding in the family!"

About the Author

ANN M. MARTIN did *a lot* of baby-sitting when she was growing up in Princeton, New Jersey. She is a former editor of books for children, and was graduated from Smith College.

Ms. Martin lives in New York City with her cats, Mouse and Rosie. She likes ice cream and *I Love Lucy*; and she hates to cook.

Ann Martin's Apple Paperbacks include *Yours Turly, Shirley*; *Ten Kids, No Pets*; *With You and Without You*; *Bummer Summer*; and all the other books in the Baby-sitters Club series.

Look for #78

CLAUDIA AND CRAZY PEACHES

Outside the air was cool and crisp. It was a perfect night for doing something wild and crazy. Peaches and I drove in her car to downtown Stoneybrook. On the way we bellowed a few more off-key choruses of, "When the moon hits your eye like a big pizza pie," at the tops of our lungs. (It was turning into our theme song.)

Pizza Express was packed with high school kids. We grabbed a table near the back corner. Then Peaches put two dollars in the juke box and told me to pick anything I wanted to hear. She ordered us a large combo deluxe pizza pie, with a side of bread sticks and marinara sauce. Then she got a soda for me and a huge chocolate milkshake for herself.

"I feel like a complete kid again," Peaches said as she happily slurped her milkshake.

I pointed out kids I recognized from Janine's

class and we made up scenarios about their lives. Then we pretended to be a dating service and paired the most unlikely kids together. Peaches and I laughed so hard that tears were streaming down our cheeks.

An hour and a half zoomed by, and before we knew it Pizza Express was closing. A guy in a white shirt and apron was stacking chairs on top of tables, while a girl was busy mopping the floor behind the counter. I looked around at the empty restaurant and got the weirdest feeling.

"Peaches?" I asked as we slipped on our jackets. "Did you leave a note for Mom?"

Peaches frowned. "Oops. I meant to, but I guess I forgot all about it."

Downtown Stoneybrook was as deserted as the restaurant. Only a few cars were parked on the street, and most of the storefronts were dark. Everything looked kind of ominous. "I hope we don't get in trouble," I muttered.

Peaches looped her arm through mine. "You worry too much. I'm sure your mom and dad are still snoring happily away in their room. They'll never even know we were gone."

"I hope you're right." But I had a sinking feeling that she was going to be wrong.

**Read all the books
about Dawn
in the Baby-sitters Club series
by Ann M. Martin**

by Ann M. Martin

More titles... ▶

The Baby-sitters Club titles continued...

Available wherever you buy books...or use this order form.

Scholastic Inc., P.O. Box 7502, 2931 E. McCarty Street, Jefferson City, MO 65102

Please send me the books I have checked above. I am enclosing $_____
(please add $2.00 to cover shipping and handling). Send check or money order - no
cash or C.O.D.s please.

Name _____ Birthdate_____

Address _____

City_____ State/Zip _____
Please allow four to six weeks for delivery. Offer good in the U.S. only. Sorry, mail orders are not
available to residents of Canada. Prices subject to change.

THE BIGGEST BSC SWEEPSTAKES EVER!

Scholastic and Ann M. Martin want to thank all of the Baby-sitters Club fans for a cool 100 million books in print! Celebrate by sending in your entry now!

ENTER AND YOU CAN WIN:

• *10 Grand Prizes:* Win one of ten $2,500 prizes!
Your cash prize is good towards any artistic, academic, or sports pursuit. Take a dance workshop, go to soccer camp, get a violin tutor, learn a foreign language! You decide and Scholastic will pay the expense up to $2,500 value. Sponsored by Scholastic Inc., the Ann M. Martin Foundation, Kid Vision, Milton Bradley® and Kenner® Products.

• *100 First Prizes:* Win one of 100 fabulous runner-up gifts selected for you by Scholastic including a limited supply of BSC videos, autographed limited editions of Ann Martin's upcoming holiday book, T-shirts, board games and other fabulous merchandise!

Just fill in the coupon below or write the information on a 3" x 5" piece of paper and mail to: **THE BSC REMEMBERS SWEEPSTAKES**, Scholastic Inc., P.O. Box 7500, 2931 East McCarty Street, Jefferson City, MO 65102. Entries must be postmarked by 10/31/94.

Send to Scholastic Inc., P.O. Box 7500, 2931 East McCarty Street, Jefferson City, MO 65102.

THE BSC REMEMBERS SWEEPSTAKES

Name _____   Birthdate _____

Address _____   Phone# _____

City _____   State _____ Zip _____

Where did you buy this book?   ❏ Bookstore   ❏ Other(Specify)

Name of Bookstore _____

BSCR19

ENTER SCHOLASTIC'S

THE BSC REMEMBERS SWEEPSTAKES

Official Rules:

No purchase necessary. To enter use the official entry form or a 3" x 5" piece of paper and hand print your full name, complete address, day telephone number and birthdate. Enter as often as you wish, one entry to an envelope. Mechanically reproduced entries are void. Mail to THE BSC REMEMBERS Sweepstakes at the address provided on the previous page, postmarked by 10/31/94. Scholastic Inc. is not responsible for late, lost or postage due mail. Sweepstakes open to residents of the U.S.A. 6-15 years old upon entering. Employees of Scholastic Inc., Kid Vision, Milton Bradley Inc., Kenner Inc., Ann M. Martin Foundation, their affiliates, subsidiaries, dealers, distributors, printers, mailers, and their immediate families are ineligible. Prize winners will be randomly drawn from all eligible entries under the supervision of Smiley Promotion Inc., an independent judging organization whose decisions are final. Prizes: Ten Grand Prizes each $2,500 awarded toward any artistic, academic or sports pursuit approved by Scholastic Inc. Winner may also choose $2,500 cash payment. An approved pursuit costing less than $2,500 must be verified by bona fide invoice and presented to Scholastic Inc. prior to 7/31/95 to receive the cash difference. One hundred First Prizes each a selection by Scholastic Inc. of BSC videos, Ann Martin books, t-shirts and games. Estimated value each $10.00. Sweepstakes void where prohibited, subject to all federal, state, provincial, local laws and regulations. Odds of winning depend on the number of entries received. Prize winners are notified by mail. Grand Prize winners and parent/legal guardian are mailed a Affidavit of Eligibility/ Liability/ Publicity/Release to be executed and returned within 14 days of its date or an alternate winner may be drawn. Only one prize allowed a person or household. Taxes on prize, expenses incurred outside of prize provision and any injury, loss or damages incurred by acceptance and use of prizes are the sole responsibility of the winners and their parent/legal guardian. Prizes cannot be exchanged, transferred or cashed. Scholastic Inc. reserves the right to substitute prizes of like value if any offered are unavailable and to use the names and likenesses of prize winners without further compensation for advertising and promotional use. Prizes that are unclaimed or undelivered to winner's address remain the property of Scholastic Inc. For a Winners List, please send a stamped, addressed envelope to THE BSC REMEMBERS Sweepstakes Winners, Smiley Promotion Inc., 271 Madison Avenue, #802, New York, N.Y. 10016 after 11/30/94. Residents of Washington state may omit return stamp.

HAVE YOU JOINED THE BSC FAN CLUB YET? See back of this book for details.

Don't miss out on The All New

Fan Club

Join now!
Your one-year membership package includes:

- The exclusive Fan Club T-Shirt!
- A Baby-sitters Club poster!
- A Baby-sitters Club note pad and pencil!
- An official membership card!
- The exclusive *Guide to Stoneybrook!*

Plus four additional newsletters per year

so you can be the first to know the hot news about the series — Super Specials, Mysteries, Videos, and more — the baby-sitters, Ann Martin, and lots of baby-sitting fun from the Baby-sitters Club Headquarters!

ALL THIS FOR JUST $6.95 plus $1.00 postage and handling! **You can't get all this great stuff anywhere else except THE BABY-SITTERS FAN CLUB!**

Just fill in the coupon below and mail with payment to: THE BABY-SITTERS FAN CLUB, Scholastic Inc., P.O. Box 7500, 2931 E. McCarty Street, Jefferson City, MO 65102.

THE BABY-SITTERS FAN CLUB

___ YES! Enroll me in The Baby-sitters Fan Club! I've enclosed my check or money order (no cash please) for $7.95

Name _____ Birthdate _____

Street _____

City _____ State/Zip _____

Where did you buy this book?

❑ Bookstore ❑ Drugstore ❑ Supermarket
❑ Book Fair ❑ Book Club ❑ other_____

BSFC593